the Case of the Haunted Health Club

CAROL FARLEY is the author of many popular books for young readers, including two previous adventures of Flee Jay and Clarice, *The Case of the Vanishing Villain,* a Children's Choice selection, and *The Case of the Lost Lookalike.* She and her family have lived in Michigan for several years.

Carol Farley has never seen a haunted health club, but she did visit a fortune teller. No one can truly know the future, she says, but she enjoys thinking about the possibilities.

the Case of the Haunted Health Club

Carol Farley

Illustrated by Tom Newsom

AN AVON  CAMELOT BOOK

THE CASE OF THE HAUNTED HEALTH CLUB is an original publication of Avon Books. This work has never before appeared in book form.

AVON BOOKS
A division of
The Hearst Corporation
105 Madison Avenue
New York, New York 10016

First Avon Camelot Printing: February 1991

CAMELOT TRADEMARK REG. U.S. PAT. OFF. AND IN OTHER COUNTRIES, MARCA REGIS-TRADA, HECHO EN U.S.A.

Printed in the U.S.A.

OPM 10 9 8 7 6 5 4 3 2 1

This book is for
Lois Scott
who tells stories
with paints and paintbrushes,
as well as with words.

Contents

Forbidden Mystery

I think I've read every mystery book in the Grand Channel Public Library. Four years ago, when I was only eight and a half, I found *And If It Melts* stuck way back on the bottom shelf of the mystery section in the children's room. Later I found out that the book was really for adults and it was there by mistake, but right then I didn't know it, and I sat down at one of the tables in the corner behind a huge potted plant and read until Miss Nesberg found me there on a last check of the library before she locked the doors and went home for the night.

"Flee Jay Saylor!" she cried. "What in the world are you reading?" She took the book and was so shocked her gray curls nearly straightened out as she flipped through the pages.

To tell you the truth, I was a little shocked myself. In fact, I had chills racing across the back of my neck even though it was a hot July day. I remember that I was so caught up in that story that I missed lunch. Maybe that doesn't mean much to you, but lunch is slightly more important to me than boys are, so you can imagine how ex-

citing that book was. I just skipped over all the words I didn't know and got to the good parts.

See, someone had killed someone and needed to find a place to hide the body. It was January, with piles and piles of snow, exactly the way it is here in Michigan every winter. The murderer decided to drag the body outside at midnight in the middle of a new snowstorm. He propped it up with a pole, and then he packed snow all around it as more snow kept falling. Soon he had made this huge fat snowman. It got colder and colder, so everything was frozen solid by morning. For weeks, the police were searching for the missing man, when there he was, standing in plain sight for the whole world to see, right inside a snowman who was smiling with a curved stick mouth and a long carrot nose. What an awful thing!

The worst thing about the book, though, was that I never found out how it ended. For months, every time I asked Miss Nesberg about it, she got all gaspy and fluttery and finally just said it was "out." So I decided to find another one just like it. I began reading every mystery book I could get my hands on. I never found one exactly like *And If It Melts*, but I did learn to love trying to put clues together in detective stories and trying to find the answers before the characters in the books did. And I made up my mind way back then that one day I would be a real detective with my own office and a secretary who would gasp and say, "My goodness, Ms. Saylor, you have a mind like a steel trap!"

My mother doesn't understand any of this. She thinks it's awful that I read so many mysteries. "Felice Jennifer," she says (she always calls me by my real name when she's being serious), "you're going to turn your brain into spaghetti."

Actually my brain might already be spaghetti because it happens to be one of my favorite foods and I eat a lot of it, but I am absolutely positive that reading mysteries doesn't numb the brain. In fact, I think they make a person smarter. You have to use your head to solve baffling puzzles, don't you? You have to keep your eyes and ears open all the time, watching what all the characters do and listening to what they say. You have to decide which ones are telling the truth and which ones aren't. You have to put all the clues together to get answers. And then—the most important thing of all—you have to have a kind of "sixth sense" when logic doesn't work.

I know all this because I used all six of my senses and solved a mystery right here in Grand Channel, just a little while ago. What was really weird is that I used an idea from that old book about the snowman when I needed a final answer. So I proved to Mom that the mysteries I have read can help me think—even if I read a particular book a long time ago, and even if it was a forbidden one. Old mysteries never die—they just lie inside your head until you need them.

Of course Clarice says *she* solved most of this case all by herself. She's my ten-year-old sister, and if her brain were half as big as she thinks it is, it would be squeezing out her ears. Still, though, I have to admit that she's bright. She's read every kind of book there is—mystery and otherwise—and she's as logical as a computer program. But, as I said, you need more than plain old facts or logic to solve some cases.

That's how it was at the Fit and Trim Health Club anyway. If you're talking about ghosts and impossible things happening, how can facts or logic help? For a while it looked as though—

But let me start at the beginning, and you can judge for yourself. Incredibly enough, it was my mother who got us all involved in this case. Which just goes to show that the best intentions of parents can often go astray. Mom got me away from reading mystery books in the safety of my own bedroom and put me into living a real mystery in a scary, haunted health club.

The Eyes of Emma

"The Fit and Trim Health Club is opening up for business again," Dad announced one Friday night at dinner. "I saw a sign in the window on the way home from work today. It said that they're giving out information and offering special rates for people who sign up before they open."

Mom's face lit up. She's attracted to sales the way I'm attracted to potato chips. She can't leave them alone and one is never enough. But this time it was more than just the thought of saving money that had her attention. "Does that mean that Emma Vickers is back in town?"

"There weren't any names listed on the sign," Dad told her. "But John Vickers owned everything on the corner of Watson Avenue and Dowland Street, didn't he? She must have inherited it all when he died. They never had any children that I know of."

"Who's Emma Vickers?" I asked. "Who's John Vickers?" But Mom and Dad were too busy talking to each other to notice me. Right away, though, my special sixth sense told me that this woman wasn't ordinary. Mom and Dad were really excited as they rattled on about her. I looked over at Clarice, but she didn't seem to be listening.

She was busy rearranging the peas on her plate into a geometric design—even her food has to be in logical order.

"People always said Emma wasn't going to come back here," Mom said. "Didn't the cold winters bother her? I wonder what happened to change her mind."

Dad laughed, and I knew he was going to make some kind of joke. Except for Clarice, everybody in our family loves puns. She doesn't like them because she says words are tools and we ought to be building solid ideas with them. I like them because you can enjoy as many as you want and they don't have any calories. "Whose mind can read a mind reader's mind?" Dad asked. "Not mine. Do you mind?"

Clarice jerked her head up. "Who's a mind reader?"

"Emma Vickers always said that she could see all and know all," Mom told her. "Past, present, and future."

"Then how come she's working at a health club?"

Mom took another sip of coffee. "Well, actually the club belonged to her husband, I guess. I don't think Emma ever had much to do with it. She was too busy with other things."

"She told people's fortunes," Dad said. "Years ago, when your mother and I were still in high school, she had a business known all over this part of the state. People came from everywhere to visit The Eyes of Emma. That's what she called her 'domain.' "

"It was a little building near the health club," Mom went on. "Torn down years ago when that diner was built. Emma would read palms or study a crystal ball. She would read cards and tea leaves. Lots of people really believed she could see the future."

It seemed like a neat thing to me. I'd love to know my

future. Will my frizzy, rusty hair be long and gorgeous one day? Will I be thin and beautiful? Will I be a great detective the way I want to be? "Could she really do it?" I asked. "Tell your exact future, I mean? Did you ever go see her, Mom?"

"Well, it was foolish, I guess, but I did. It only cost a few dollars. I had her read my palm just before I graduated."

"And did she get anything right about your future?"

Mom threw a quick look at Dad and they both laughed. "She was right on the button," Mom said. "Emma told me that I would marry a light stranger and have piles of money."

"But you knew Daddy all your life," Clarice blurted. "You went all through school together, and he's the only one you ever married. He wasn't a stranger."

"Well, he gets stranger and stranger every day, doesn't he?" Mom asked.

Clarice didn't get the joke. "And he's dark," she added. "Daddy and Flee Jay both have dark hair."

"But I'm light on my feet," Dad said, jumping up to do a quick tap dance. "See that?"

"And Mom's got piles of money in the bank where she works," I said, getting into the fun. "So that fortune-teller was right about all three things!"

Clarice frowned. "Anybody can say anything about the future, then, and somebody will think the prediction was right."

"That's how fortune-tellers work, honey," Mom explained. "They make vague statements that could mea: just about anything. Some people are so eager to know what

8

the future holds that they latch on to anything that makes the least bit of sense. Emma Vickers wore strange clothes and mumbled mysterious words when she looked at our palms years ago. We were just kids then, and we all thought she had some kind of special powers.''

"Well, she did put on a good show," Dad said. "The owners of the Old Time Circus thought so too. They hired her to star in their traveling show. So she and John closed up the health club and left Grand Channel around ten years ago. It was big news here. Small town folks make good in show business—that sort of thing. Then we didn't hear much about them until around six months ago when we saw in the newspaper that John Vickers had had a heart attack and died. Now it looks as though his old health club is opening up again."

Mom got all dreamy-eyed. "I wonder if Emma is there. Wouldn't it be fun to see her, Ron? I'd guess that she's close to seventy by now. Don't you think so? When we last saw her, she must have been—" Suddenly she stopped. "Say! I just had a great idea! Why don't we find out about joining the club? They probably will be having aerobic classes and exercise equipment. We could all use that. And they probably will have special family rates. I've been thinking lately that the girls don't—"

"I don't want to join a health club," Clarice interrupted. "Flee Jay can do it."

I had a quick vision of myself jumping around in a leotard, and the picture gave me the heebie-jeebies. "Nope, not me."

"Well, I'm not fat," Clarice said. "But Flee Jay—"

I glared at her. "Well neither am I! I may not be as

skinny as you are, but I'm almost a teenager, and teenagers need fat."

"Not where you've got it," Clarice said.

Mom spoke before I could zing back an answer. "Girls! That's enough. Health clubs aren't just for people who are overweight. They're for people who want to stay healthy."

"But didn't you just say the owner of that health club died of a heart attack?" Clarice asked.

There were a couple of seconds of silence as Dad and Mom looked at each other. They're proud that Clarice is so bright, I guess, but sometimes they get stymied too. Just like me.

Finally Dad cleared his throat. "John Vickers was an old man. Maybe if he hadn't worked out in his health club, he would have died lots sooner." He glanced at me. "Why not make your mother happy by riding your bikes over there Monday morning to get some information? The sign said that someone would be there to answer questions all day every day. After we find out more, we can decide whether we want to join."

Mom stood up. "And you might enjoy meeting Emma Vickers if she's there now. She's a real character."

Clarice sniffed. "Well I think all this business about seeing into the future is dumb. What's so special about it? Anybody with any brains can do it. I can do it myself."

I felt my ears perk up. Clarice is a genius, no doubt about that. But nobody is smart enough to actually see into the future. "Hah!" I said. "That's a laugh."

She blinked her big blue eyes at me. "Want me to tell

you exactly what your future holds, Flee Jay? I'll bet you a quarter I can do it."

"*Exactly* what my future holds?"

"Exactly."

I sat back and folded my arms. This was going to be easy. For once in my life I would be getting the better of my sister, and I'd win a quarter in the bargain. "Can Mom be the judge to agree if you're right or wrong?"

"Sure."

"Okay, then. You're on."

Clarice waved her hands around and made her voice all creepy sounding. "You're going to stand up. You're going to clear this table, and you're going to do the dishes."

"What?" I shoved my chair back. "What kind of future is that?"

Mom laughed. "She's got you, Flee Jay. It's your turn to do the kitchen tonight. Clarice did it last night."

"But I thought that the future meant—"

"The future is what happens after the present." Smiling, Clarice pushed a pile of dishes toward me. "Get busy, big sister."

"Don't forget to do the coffeepot," Mom called as she and Dad left for the living room.

Clarice stood up to leave too. She grinned and leaned closer to me. "Nanny, nanny, boo, boo, I'm smarter than you you," she whispered.

Oh, how I hate it when she says those words! I grabbed the sponge and threw it at her, but she was already out of the kitchen.

Still, though, I had learned a good lesson—no more bets with Clarice, no matter how sure they seemed.

. And I learned something else. I vowed never to have my fortune told. As I stood there scouring pots and pans, I realized that knowing your exact future doesn't always bring happiness.

A Body in the
Fit and Trim Health Club

"Now be sure to find out if they have special rates for families," Mom told us on Monday morning. "And if Emma Vickers is there, be sure you tell her who your parents are."

"I'm going to tell her that she got your fortune all wrong too," Clarice said.

Mom laughed. "But we sure have had fun making jokes about it all these years."

"What jokes?" Clarice asked.

After Mom left for work, she went into a long lecture about how it's impossible to really see into the future, but I wasn't really listening to most of it. Clarice's lectures are a lot like soap operas—there's a lot you may not really care about hearing, and even if you miss half, you can still tell what's going on. To tell you the truth, I was really eager to meet this Emma Vickers, and I was hoping that she would be the one opening up the health club again.

By 9:30, Clarice and I were thumping and bumping up and down curbs on our way to Watson Avenue. It was a hot August day, and my bike doesn't have any fancy gears.

Soon I was huffing and puffing so hard that I decided I'd be so fit and trim by the time I reached the health club that I wouldn't even need to go inside.

As usual, Clarice was leading the way, her long blonde hair waving out behind her. She makes riding a bike look easy. I knew that her pink shorts and blouse wouldn't even be smudged with dirt or sweat when we got there. Her ugly black purse was slung over her shoulder, bulging from everything she had stuffed inside. Besides the quarter I'd had to pay her after our bet on Friday night, it contained disinfectant, pencils, and notebooks. The notebooks were so full of heavy facts that I wondered why the tires on her bike didn't go flat from all the extra weight. The rhinestones on the purse handle caught the glare of the sun and dazzled my eyes. I could only hope that the bright light didn't stop traffic.

Actually, I guess there wasn't enough traffic to worry about. Grand Channel is a small town and we were riding on the east side, away from Lake Michigan, where all the good stores and restaurants are. Nobody would have much reason to spend time on the streets we traveled. The farther we moved along Watson Avenue, the worse everything looked. We passed a ramshackle gas station, two deserted warehouses, and an old empty diner. When we reached the corner of Watson and Dowland, I saw a dilapidated two-story building.

Clarice stopped her bike. "You suppose this is it?"

I pulled up beside her and looked around. There was a small park across the street, and it looked clean and neat, but everything in front of us was a mess. The building itself sure didn't *look* like a health club. The paint was peeling off its bricks, shingles were hanging down from the roof, and the front window was cracked. Dirt and garbage were piled up against the sides of the building, and old newspapers and paper cups littered the steps. Only the big sign in the huge front window convinced me that we were at the right place.

THE FIT AND TRIM HEALTH CLUB
WILL BE OPENING AGAIN SOON!!
REDUCED RATES!
ASK ABOUT OUR PLANS!
OPEN NOW FOR QUESTIONS—STOP IN
MON—FRI   10:00—6:00

Clarice climbed off her bike. Staring up at the crumbling building, she shook her head. "They gave this place the wrong name," she said. "There's nothing fit and trim about this building, that's for sure."

I leaned my bike up against a lamp post and moved over to the window. The big paper sign blocked most of the view, but by standing up on my toes, I could see a bit over the top. I wiped the sweat off my forehead and peered inside. The place looked bleak and empty. "There aren't any lights on," I said. "It's all deserted. Maybe nobody's in there."

Clarice moved over beside me. She was too short to see over the paper banner, but she pointed at the words. "The sign says they're open for questions."

"Then maybe we got here too early."

"It's nearly ten-thirty." Clarice turned from the window. "Let's try the door."

Usually I'm the one trying to get *her* to do something. But this time I held back. The place looked so creepy and strange that I had weird vibrations about it. "It's probably locked," I said. "Let's just go home and tell Mom nobody was here."

Clarice waved at the sign again. "But if they say someone is here to answer questions, then somebody ought to be here," she declared.

Clarice has always had a lot more faith in what she reads than I have. Reluctantly I tagged behind her as she moved to the entrance. The window there was grimy and smudged. The wood was gouged and chipped. At one time the brass handle had been shiny, maybe, but now it was green and black. "See? I'll bet it hasn't been opened in years and years."

"But the sign says—" Clarice took a deep breath and touched the dirty handle. She hates germs, but sometimes her curiosity makes her forget about them. Still, she grimaced when her fingers touched the metal. With a low creaking sound, the door slowly swung open.

For a few seconds we just stood there blinking. The area stretching out in front of us was dark, dingy, and full of cobwebs. The odor of dust clung to the walls and to the ugly brown carpet. Except for a few folding chairs, the room was almost empty. A long wooden desk stretched to the left, and a pile of papers lay at one end. Old yellowed papers were tacked up on a bulletin board behind it. Cobwebs hung from the ceiling and in the corners of the walls. There was a large, hand-printed sign on one of the four doors leading from the room. It said JUCUZZI.

Clarice stared at it. "I don't think that's spelled right."

If they spelled a word wrong in her obituary, Clarice would jump out of her coffin to make the correction. Sighing, I brushed a few cobwebs that were hanging from the ceiling. "Maybe only spiders keep fit and trim in here."

"Well, I'm going to—"

I grabbed the back of her blouse. "Don't go all the way in! Can't you see? Nobody's here!"

"I want to see what those papers on the desk say," she told me, jerking away. "Maybe they're pamphlets telling all about the club. Remember? We promised Mom we'd get some information, didn't we?"

"But—" I hesitated. My sixth sense was jumping up all over the place. I wanted to run, but I was curious too. "All right then," I said, "all right! But let's stick together. I'm not sure if this is trespassing or what."

Together we moved closer to the huge long desk. "Nothing much here," I started to say, glancing over the dusty surface. But Clarice gave a funny yelp before I could finish.

"Look, Flee Jay! Look!"

I yelped too. Clarice was pointing at a small dark heap lying sprawled out on the floor.

Like a dummy, I stood there staring for a second before I realized what we were looking at. It was the body of a dark-haired woman. She was lying face down, with a purple and silver robe almost completely covering her.

I threw my hands over my face. In television shows people always scream when they find a dead body, but I was too terrified to make a sound. I stood there staring, too scared to move. I know all about CPR and I even know the Heimlich Manuever. But all of that business flew right out of my head. Like a real dummy, I just stood there while

Clarice went running over. She knelt down by the body of the woman.

"Is she dead?" I asked. My voice sounded all croaky, and my neck had chills. "Is she dead, Clarice?"

Poisoned?

"Dead!" A hoarse voice sounded behind me. The lights flashed on and a blur streaked past as a tall skinny man went dashing over to the woman. "Oh no! Aunt Emma? Aunt Emma?"

The figure on the floor moved. Nobody was dead after all. I sagged in relief. Now I saw that the woman wasn't dark-haired either—she was wearing a black turban. Her dress was a long robe covered with silver designs. She groaned and opened her eyes.

"Are you okay?" Clarice asked, leaning over the woman. "Are you okay?"

"What happened?" the man shouted, bending closer. His voice cracked, almost like some of the boys' in my class, and that's when I realized that he wasn't very old, even though he had a straggly brown beard. His hair was in a ponytail, and he was wearing a Michigan State sweat shirt. "What happened, Aunt Emma?"

The woman ran her hands across her face. She had enormous rings and long purple fingernails. At last my paralyzed brain started working again, and the strange costume made sense to me. This had to be the famous Emma Vickers! I moved closer. "Are you sick?"

Blinking, she sat up and stared around. "Are you here already, Emmett? What time is it? What time is it?"

Even in the midst of terrible emergencies, Clarice knows the answers. "Ten-thirty."

"Half an hour!" Emma Vickers grabbed at the side of the desk. "Oh my! I've been lying here for half an hour!"

"But what happened, Aunt Emma?" As the man stared at her, his long thin face seemed as white and green as his sweat shirt. Some of the long hair from his ponytail had come loose, and it hung around his face. He'd hardly even looked at me or Clarice.

"Are you Emma Vickers?" Clarice asked.

"Yes. Yes, I am, dear." Shakily, she stood up. Even at her full height she wasn't much taller than Clarice. She was short and plump, with a round face covered with heavy makeup. She might have been over seventy, the way Mom had said, but it was hard to tell, because she didn't look like any other old woman I've ever seen. Her cheeks had two rosy circles and her eyelids were purple. She had a black beauty mark on her chin and was wearing a long silver necklace. Her black turban fitted tightly around her face. The designs on her robe—planets, stars, and zodiac signs—were a shiny metal. Her voice was low and hoarse; it made everything she said seem like a mysterious secret. Slowly she sank down on to the chair beside the desk. "Well, Emmett, I had just taken a few sips, when suddenly—"

"Was it the iced tea again?" Frowning, Emmett pointed to the empty plastic glass lying on the floor a few feet ahead of the place we had found Mrs. Vickers. There was a huge wet stain spreading out away from the rim of the glass. "Didn't you drink the tea I made? Nobody could have put anything inside that container without breaking the seal I put on that lid."

Mrs. Vickers patted her turban down around her face and began to poke wisps of gray hair up under it. Leaning back against the chair, she took a deep breath. "Now, Emmett, I've told you before. If the spirits want to make trouble, you can't stop them. Yes, I did drink the tea you made. It was closed inside the container exactly the way you left it. I put a few ice cubes in my glass, poured in the tea, and sat down to drink it just before ten o'clock. I wanted to be ready to start giving out information the way we said we would do today. But—"

"It must have been the ice cubes!" Emmett stood up straighter. "Maybe someone put something in the ice cubes! I'll get the tray, that's what I'll do. I'll have those ice cubes analyzed at a laboratory. One way or another, we'll get to the bottom of this. It's a sure thing spirits weren't involved here, but *somebody* may have tried to poison you again."

"Poison!" Clarice and I blurted the word out at the same instant. Obviously startled, the other two turned to stare at us.

I wondered if Clarice and I looked as different from each other as they did. He was tall and skinny, and the hair on his head and in his beard stuck out in all directions. She was short and round, with no hair showing. He was wearing jeans and a sweat shirt, clothes you see on people every day, and she was wearing things that most people wear only to a costume party. They were standing there talking about spirits and poison the way Clarice and I might talk about movies and popcorn.

"Who're you?" Emmett demanded, as though he had just realized that we were there.

I swallowed and was embarrassed that the sound seemed so loud in the huge empty room. "I'm Flee Jay Saylor, and this is my sister, Clarice. We came—"

"You came because your mother wondered about me," Mrs. Vickers finished. There was a tinkling sound, and I noticed that her necklace was a chain of small metal bells which rattled when she moved. Her deep voice grew louder and more mysterious. "I read her palm years ago when she was in high school and now she wanted to find out if I was here opening up my husband's old health club. She wondered about the special prices for family rates too." She stopped. Her purple eyelids fluttered. "Is this not so, my dears?"

I caught my breath. "How did you—"

"The spirits tell me, child. The spirits help me see all and know all. And now they've been warning me to leave this place, leave it all for my nephew here and—"

"The spirits *don't* poison people," her nephew declared. "I told you that yesterday. Something crazy is going on around here, Aunt Emma, and I want to get to the bottom of it. Somebody may be trying to scare us away. Yesterday you were sick after drinking iced tea, so you thought those spirits of yours were trying to scare you away. Today, when you drank from a fresh batch—one I made myself—we find you flat on the floor. But there's no way there could be any poison in that tea! If there was poison, it was in the ice cubes!"

24

Mrs. Vickers waved her hands. The rings on her fingers glittered. "But the spirits can—"

The young man whirled around. "Where's the rest of the ice cubes? That's the only way to prove to you that—" Mumbling and frowning, he stomped out of the main room, his ponytail flapping against his sweat shirt.

Mrs. Vickers made another sweeping gesture with her arms, and her huge sleeves drooped and fluttered. She stood up again and leaned against the side of the desk. "You poor, poor children! You must have been frightened right out of your wits! My nephew—he's the son of my late husband's brother—why, he—"

"What happened to the rest of the ice cubes?" Emmett Vickers demanded as he came back into the room again. "There's just an empty tray on the counter."

"Why, I just used a few in my glass and then I dumped the rest in the sink so I could wash out the tray a bit. I never thought a thing about it. There's another tray of ice cubes in the freezer, you know, dear."

Emmett frowned. "But now we won't have any proof that somebody—"

"Child, child," Mrs. Vickers said. "What proof do we need? The spirits are trying to tell us something. It's perfectly clear. Perfectly clear. They're sending me a warning. They want me away so you can take over and have this whole building for yourself."

"Oh, rubbish, Aunt Emma!"

Clarice was looking at the stains on the floor. "You must have dropped this glass straight down when you fell. Is that right?" She bent over and ran her hands forward along the carpet.

Her actions didn't surprise me in the least. After all, Clarice has been known to stand in bathroom sinks to reach air vents so she can eavesdrop on conversations in other rooms. On the path to better understanding, Clarice will do just about anything.

But Emmett Vickers obviously didn't like what he saw. "Hey now, what do you think you're doing? Who are you kids anyway?"

"Now, now, Emmett." Mrs. Vickers touched her nephew's arm. "Don't be so cranky." She turned and beamed at Clarice and me, and her voice grew high and chirpy. "Why, they're detectives, that's what they are, and they're here to help me."

I heard a gasp, but I really don't know whether it came from Clarice or me. We both were staring at the woman who had told us her "spirits" helped her see and know "all." Emma Vickers modestly patted her black turban and fluttered her purple eyelids.

An Amazing Offer

My thoughts were whirling. Nobody in all of Grand Channel thinks of us as detectives. The kids in school would howl at such a crazy idea. To everybody in the world I'm just plain old Felice Jennifer Saylor, Dull Person. How had Emma Vickers known that Clarice and I had solved some mysteries?

She had been right about what Mom had said too. Maybe she *did* have some kind of special power. And if her "spirits" could tell her about other people's lives, then maybe they could think of a way to poison her, too. But would they really want to hurt her? My ideas were jumping around like rubber ducks in a jacuzzi. (Yeah, the word *was* spelled wrong on their sign. Clarice was right once again.)

She hugged her purse closer to her side. "How'd you know about us?" she asked.

Mrs. Vickers waved her hands, and her necklace bells clinked. She lowered her voice. "Why, the spirits told me, my dear. They're all around us, all around us. I'm in constant touch with another world. An invisible world."

I looked around the room again, half expecting to find ghostly figures wafting and whispering. But except for the desk and the few folding chairs, the room was still empty. Now that the lights were on, I saw more dust and grime. The old brown carpet was worn, and there were layers and layers of dirt everywhere. It looked as though the place had just been opened up after years of being locked and forgotten. I wondered if the closed doors led to other rooms that were as empty as this one was. Maybe spirits were flittering and gossiping in one of those rooms.

"Spirits don't really exist," Clarice declared. "No one has ever proved scientifically that they do."

The bells tinkled and little Mrs. Vickers frowned. "Science, schmience! Proof? Schmoof! Didn't you ever hear of the 'Eyes of Emma'? I have powers greater than earthly powers. Why, I had my own little building because so many people wanted to visit me. They came from all over the country to talk to me. The spirits told me what to say. Isn't that right, Emmett? Isn't that right?"

Emmett Vickers had picked up the plastic glass. He put it on the desk. "That's what I've heard," he said. "But that little building has been gone a long time, Aunt Emma. 'The Eyes of Emma' was replaced by that diner at least ten years ago when Uncle John sold the land over there. And now it's as run-down as this place is." He glanced over at the dirty windows, and his shoulders slumped. "We'll need to do a lot of work here before we can get this club back into shape. I don't know why Uncle John—"

"But you can do it all right, Emmett! You can—"

"*We* can," Emmett interrupted. "Uncle John wanted both of us to take over this health club, didn't he? And once we find out that there's enough interest around here, we'll get started." He came closer and hovered over her. "Are you really okay now, Aunt Emma? Really?"

"It was only a warning, dear. The spirits are trying to show you that this place ought to be yours alone. They—"

Jerking upright, he shook his head. "No, I don't think there was any kind of warning from 'spirits.' But maybe you had one from Crandell Teeters. He's the one I'm worrying about. He's not from any unreal world, and he sure isn't invisible! He's real!"

Clarice's ears perked up. I didn't actually see them wiggle, but I could tell by the sound of her voice that she suddenly had new interest. "Isn't he the man who just moved here from Chicago? The one who drives around in that big white Cadillac?"

Emmett nodded. "He's been in, wanting us to sell this building to him. Been here twice, in fact. Says he wants to run his own health club." His voice grew louder, and his beard almost bristled. "We told him no. After all, Uncle John's will said that he wanted the two of us to run this place. Old Teeters nearly flipped his lid when I told him to forget it. Guess he's not used to having anybody say no to him."

"He thought we'd be eager to sell now that John's gone," Mrs. Vickers said. She paused and her eyes filled with tears. She blinked them away. "But Mr. Teeters wasn't willing to pay half the value of this place, and Emmett needs money for his future. He may even go to college! But no, Emmett, he hasn't been back. Don't worry about him so much. I've told you and told you that these mishaps for me are just warnings from the spirit world so that I'll leave here and let you handle—"

Emmett whirled around and started off before she could finish. "I'm going out back to do some work. These kids need information about the health club, so go ahead and tell them what we're planning. Detectives! Ha! That shows you how much those 'spirits' of yours know. I'll bet these two couldn't find their way out of a paper bag!" The door banged behind him.

Clarice silently stared after him. All the facts inside her head and her purse must have been throbbing. I was amazed that she didn't march off and tell him about her fabulous IQ, which is nearly as high as the national debt. But she just adjusted the strap on her purse and hugged it tighter to her side.

"That looks heavy, dear," Mrs. Vickers said. "Would you like to put it up here on the desk while I tell you about our health club plan?"

"No," Clarice told her. "No, thank you."

Mrs. Vickers cocked her head to one side. "Few children carry a purse like that. One so full of notebooks. But then you need them to write down all those facts, I guess, and that's why it's so valuable to you. I'm curious why you keep disinfectant in there, though, dear. What do you do with that?"

Clarice's mouth dropped open, and maybe mine did too. Clarice always carries disinfectant in her purse so that she can use it in public restrooms. Like I've told you, she's afraid of germs. She even flushes gas station toilets with her foot so she doesn't have to touch the handle. But how could Mrs. Vickers have known she carries around something so weird?

She didn't seem to notice how surprised we were. Maybe

30

she was used to having people gape at her after one of her announcements. She swirled around and marched behind the desk, and tried to look very business-like despite her peculiar outfit.

"Well now, what we're doing is taking names. We're handing out these sheets of information to people who ask about our program. As we get more and more names, we'll order more and more equipment so that our clients will have the best health club available." She paused and glanced around the empty room. "You can see we're not even close to being ready to open yet. We need to know there's enough interest before we order all those expensive machines."

"How come you don't know that already?" Clarice asked. "Can't you look in the future and see if you'll make a lot of money here?"

Now it was Mrs. Vickers's turn to gape. Her wrinkled face puckered. Then she sighed. "Alas, no, my child. I cannot. The spirits can never be used for great personal gain." She took a deep breath and gestured again. "John sold all our old machines when we left here. It may not look like much now, but this place could be one of the finest health clubs in the state. Emmett could make a fortune here. I plan to tell everybody who comes in that this will be a good bargain for them. People need good exercise programs if they want to be fit and healthy, and . . ." Her voice faded as she looked down at her billowing robe. "But I guess I'm not a very good advertisement for this place, am I?"

That was exactly what I'd been thinking. I felt my face flush. Good grief, she really *could* read minds. I wriggled the skin on my forehead to make sure it hadn't turned to glass so that people could look inside my head and see my thoughts. I'd been visualizing all those health club commercials on TV. The people there are gorgeous, tanned, and skinny. They wear tight leotards and talk about yogurt and aerobics. Little Mrs. Vickers just didn't fit the picture. Her talk about invisible spirits made more sense than her talk about keeping fit and healthy. It was strange to see her rattling on about health plans while she blinked her purple eyelids and patted down her black turban. It was weird to hear her necklace bells tinkling while she talked, to watch her long flapping sleeves sparkle with their silver symbols when she waved her arms.

I curled my toes inside my sandals and looked down at the floor. It was okay for me to think those thoughts, but I didn't like having her *know* what I was thinking.

"In any case," she went on, "we can assure clients that we'll have prices ten percent lower than any other place in town once we open for business. Tell your parents that, children, and see if they feel they'd like to belong to this club once everything is in tiptop shape." She leaned away from the desk. "Now, then, back to the two of you. Even if your parents aren't interested in the health club plan, would the two of you like to help us?"

Clarice eagerly perked up "Find out about the poison, you mean?"

Mrs. Vickers laughed. "No, no, not that. I know about that, my dear. I don't need a detective for that. It was the spirits, that's what. Maybe they put a little something in the ice cubes to get my attention. The spirits wouldn't actually harm me. They're merely warning me away. They want Emmett to have this place all for himself.''

Sighing, she looked down and brushed at some dust on the top of the desk. ''No, what I meant by needing help is that we want someone to clean the rooms and organize the few things John left in storage here. You two girls might be just the ones. We need the windows washed and the carpet vacuumed, the place swept, and the shelves cleaned. We need the cobwebs and the dust cleared away and the closets in each of the back rooms cleaned. We could pay you each three dollars an hour to help us this week. Even if I leave—especially if I leave—Emmett will want this place clean. What do you think? Would the two of you like the job? What do you think?''

I had lots of thoughts, but I wasn't sure I wanted Mrs. Vickers to know them. I talked extra loud so that my voice would drown out what was going on inside my head. I wasn't absolutely sure she could read my mind, but I didn't want to take any chances.

''We'll ask our parents,'' I told her, not giving Clarice a chance to answer. ''We'll go home and ask our parents.'' I grabbed Clarice's arm and half pulled her out the door.

Great Potential

"What's the big idea?" Clarice demanded when we were blinking in the bright sunlight again. "You didn't have to grab me that way. Look, you got dirt on my shirt."

I moved toward our bicycles. "Come on—I wanted to talk to you before you answered Mrs. Vickers. I know you, and I know exactly what you were going to do. You were going to refuse that job, weren't you? You hate dirt. You hate germs. You hate dust. You don't like ideas where logic won't work. You were going to tell Mrs. Vickers that we didn't want to work in there. But I want to! There's a real mystery going on in that health club, and I want to solve it. This could be a great case for me. I could—"

Clarice sidled on to her bike. "That's how much *you* know, Ms. Felice Jennifer, the Mind Reader. I was going to say yes. I want to get some answers too."

"But—"

"I do hate all those things," she went on. "You're right about that. But I like using logic too. And I like finding answers to puzzles as much as you do. There are more mysterious things going on in that place than you could even guess. I want to find some answers."

I could hardly believe my ears. "Then you *do* think somebody tampered with those ice cubes the way Emmett Vickers said?" I lowered my voice. "You really think that some kind of spirits may be sending Mrs. Vickers a warning?"

"*Somebody's* sending a warning or a message to somebody, all right. But there aren't any mysterious spirits or ghosts floating around. Somebody human is trying to make trouble. I already saw a logical clue about those ice cubes, and I know that clue wasn't from the 'spirit world.' "

"A clue!" I was so surprised, my voice cracked. "But I was right in there with you all the time. I didn't see a clue!"

"Well, it was there. Plain as can be to anybody who stops and thinks." Clarice waved her hand as she started off. "Nanny, nanny, boo, boo," she called back. "You can't do what I do."

The words zinged back like disgusting little bees. They were annoying and they stung. Wasn't I supposed to be the detective here? If Clarice had seen a real clue, she ought to have told me about it. I furiously pedaled to catch up with her so I could tell her what I thought, but by the time I reached her, I was too winded and too mad to talk. I decided to punish her by not speaking to her for the rest of the day.

But, later that afternoon, I had to give up my vow. I'd been thinking and thinking about the things Mrs. Vickers had said. It made me feel all spooky when I thought about how right she'd been so many times. I wondered what Clarice thought about that. Besides, I knew we would need Mom and Dad's permission before we could take that job, so I wanted to give her some advice about how we should ask. Clarice always jumps into conversations the way little kids jump into mud puddles: both feet flying. She spouts out facts and figures until they splash all over. But sometimes—especially with parents—you need to think more about emotions and less about facts.

"Mom and Dad get all excited and worried about nothing," I told Clarice just before dinner time. She was busy scribbling in her notebook. "We'd better not mention the way we found Mrs. Vickers today. Okay?"

She looked up from her notebook. "I wasn't going to."

"We won't talk about spirits or poison or anything like that either. I've been thinking of the things we ought to emphasize. Let's be sure to mention that park across the street. Maybe we can eat there. Mom and Dad are always telling us we need to get outside more often." As I spoke, I walked closer, stretching my neck, trying to see what she had been writing, but she flipped her notebook closed.

I pretended I just wanted to look at the plant near her chair. "Hmmmm, I guess this doesn't need water after all," I mumbled. I looked at her again. "I've been thinking, though. Mrs. Vickers was right about a lot of things today, wasn't she?"

"I guess so."

"Well, I know you said there aren't any spirits. Maybe there are and maybe there aren't. I guess spirits don't seem very logical. But since Mrs. Vickers was right about so many things, don't you think it might be possible to read people's minds and see their past and future?"

"No."

"No? But you just admitted that Mrs. Vickers was right

36

about a lot of things. She knew exactly what our parents had said to us, for instance.''

Clarice tapped her pencil against her chin. ''I think it was just logic, Flee Jay,'' she said, leaning closer. ''I've just been writing about that. Everything Mrs. Vickers said about us would be true for just about any kid our age who lives in Grand Channel. People who knew Emma Vickers from her 'Eyes of Emma' place would send their kids over to ask about the health club. We're just about the right age to have parents who would have been in high school when she was so famous around here. And all families with two kids would want to know about special rates.''

''But what about your purse? She knew exactly what you had inside it.''

''I sat it right down by her face when I got down on the floor to talk to her. Remember? I figured that out too. She could easily have seen the pencils and notebooks sticking out. And isn't anything you write a fact?'' Clarice wrinkled up her nose. ''I mean, I might have been writing down the names of boys I like, and that might have been a bunch of facts too. See, the things she said were all kind of vague, so they sounded right on target no matter who heard them.''

''But the disinfectant?''

''Maybe she smelled it. My gosh, Flee Jay, don't look so disappointed! You look as sad as you looked the day I told you there wasn't really a Santa Claus.''

I glared at her. ''You never told me that! I knew a whole year before you did!'' She laughed, so I knew that was her idea of a joke. Like I've said before—Clarice doesn't have much of a sense of humor. I folded my arms. ''How'd Mrs. Vickers know we were detectives, then?''

Clarice looked back down at her book. "I was down on my knees examining the carpet, wasn't I? And I was asking her a question right before she said that. Wouldn't anybody guess that you and I were trying to be detectives?"

I bit my tongue. I hadn't been going to ask any more questions, but I was willing to give up my pride in order to get one more answer. "And that clue you were talking about? The one about the ice cubes. When are you going to tell me about it?"

"When I know more," she said. "But you could figure it out yourself if you thought about it long enough. Just think about what we saw and heard in there today."

I racked my brain until dinner time trying to figure out what Clarice had seen or heard that had escaped me, but I finally had to give up. I vowed I'd get her to tell me the answer when we went to the club the next day. "Don't forget," I whispered to her as we sat down at the table. "Don't tell Mom and Dad about the weird stuff that happened at the health club. We don't want to shock them."

But as it turned out, they were shocked anyway by the time I finished telling them about our job offer.

"Well, frankly, I'm surprised," Dad said, staring at us. "I sure never would have guessed that you two girls would want a clean-up job like that."

"I can hardly get Flee Jay to clean up her room," Mom put in. She looked at me. "Has Emma Vickers changed into a sweet old lady? Was she wearing angel wings? Did she use some magical power on you?"

"She was wearing a black turban and a long robe with metal zodiac signs," I said. "She had purple eyelids and a

38

black beauty mark. She waved her hands a lot and talked about her special powers.''

Mom laughed. "So then she hasn't changed a bit. She still puts on quite a show. But I'm surprised you'd want to spend a lot of time with her. Especially you, Clarice. Her ideas aren't very logical, are they?''

Clarice smiled her Miss Innocent smile. "It's sort of a new experience for me.''

Mom and Dad were struck speechless. I guess it must have been a shock for them to hear her sweetly repeating their own words. They're always telling her to get away from her books and find some new experiences in the world.

"We thought we could do something nice for an old friend of yours,'' I quickly added while we were on a roll. "She seemed to know a lot about you.''

Mom looked pleased. "She remembered us, then? Well. Well, then.''

Dad cleared his throat. "But can you two girls be much help? It sounds to me as though there's a lot of work to do before they can open that club. And how'll you get back and forth? What about lunch?''

"Emmett Vickers will do all the heavy work,'' I said. "He's her nephew. Clarice and I will just sweep and clean and sort things out. We'll ride our bikes there. We'll be outside in the fresh air all that time. And we can carry our lunches and eat in the little park across the street from the club. We'll only be helping out for a few days. Can we go there tomorrow to work for a while and tell her that you'll join the club when everything's set?''

"Well, what about your appointment at the dentist on Wednesday?'' Mom asked me.

I groaned. My thoughts about dental appointments always vanish before they hit my brain. "Well, the dentist's office isn't far from there. I'll ride my bike there and back."

"It would be a good chance for us to see how it feels to have a real job," Clarice added.

Mom laughed. "Sounds like they really want to go to work, Ron. Let's give them a chance to see life in the real world."

"Well, maybe for a few days." Dad nodded. "I guess it will be all right, girls."

"Go ahead and say that we'd be willing to join the club if the rates are truly going to be lower than anywhere else," Mom said. "And tell Emma Vickers that we'll try to get in to see her sometime soon."

"No need to hurry!" I answered quickly. I couldn't even imagine what would happen if they ever walked in and found Emma Vickers flat on the floor the way we had.

Health clubs, it seemed, could be hazardous to your health.

Nobody Human

A long white Cadillac was pulling away from the curb when we reached the health club the next morning. As my bike clunked to a stop behind Clarice's, I stared at the license plate on the car. A good detective has to notice things like that. "Somebody rich must want to be fit and trim too," I said.

Clarice neatly balanced her bike on the kickstand, then she locked the tires with a pink band. As usual, I had forgotten my lock. She smoothed down her white shorts. "He could afford to lose about forty pounds, I'd say. Maybe even fifty."

"Who could?" I crammed my bike up against the building. Nobody would want to steal anything so banged up, I told myself, marveling that Clarice and I had both received our bikes on the same day. Hers was as shiny and bright as it had been in the window of Sears. Mine looked as though it had gone through the trash masher in their back alley.

"Crandell Teeters," she told me. "He's the one who owns that car you were just staring at. I've seen him

driving around town lots of times in there, all scrunched down in the backseat. Probably eating potato chips. I saw him in the 7–11 buying a huge bag last week, in fact. Yuck!''

I love potato chips, but I didn't try to defend them. Clarice can't stand anything that crumbles and makes a mess. Personally, I don't think we should judge food on how easily you can wrap it up and carry it in a big purse full of notebooks.

She took her purse with her healthful, neat lunch packed inside, and lifted it from her bike basket. I had my junk lunch all crammed inside a book bag. "Maybe he came to talk about buying the club again," Clarice went on.

"Well, if we ever need his license number, I've got it memorized," I told her, hurrying toward the door. "My mind is like a steel trap."

"And usually just as empty," Clarice said, grinning. She had opened the door and was inside before I could come up with a snappy answer.

Emmett and Mrs. Vickers didn't hear us, because they were by the desk busily talking as we came in. At least Emmett was talking. Mrs. Vickers, in a green turban and tight black sweat suit, which seemed even more peculiar than the robe she had worn the day before, seemed to be doing nothing but listening. Her rouged face was all crinkled up, her green eyelids were blinking, and her purple lips were pursed together as she watched Emmett waving his arms and shouting.

"You shouldn't have told Mr. Teeters about those crazy 'spirits' of yours, Aunt Emma! Those 'entities' or whatever it is you call them! The offer he made for this building was low enough—after those stories, he'll probably think he can offer even less!''

"Now, Emmett," Mrs. Vickers said, blinking her eyes and reaching out her hand. I noticed that her long painted fingernails had disappeared today. "Now, Emmett, I only said—"

"You told him the spirits were sending warnings that you should leave this place. You said they were doing all sorts of weird stuff.''

"But he asked how things were, didn't he? I only told him what was really happening.''

Emmett heaved a huge sigh. His Michigan State sweatshirt rose up and fell flat on his skinny chest. "But you've given him a reason to offer even less money for this property! Don't you see that? Maybe if he came up with a decent offer, we *would* sell.''

"Oh, no, Emmett. You must be joking! John meant for you to have this club. I keep telling you that. You need the income so you can start college, don't you? Once this club gets going, why, you'll make more money than anything that tightwad Crandell Teeters would offer! The spirits want me out of here so that you can carry out John's plans.''

Emmett folded his arms. "And I suppose they don't like Crandell Teeters?''

Mrs. Vickers frowned. "No, they don't. And neither do I. I don't trust that man. He has a bad aura. He gives off bad vibrations, that's what. Those bulging eyes of his—that smirky grin. And that awful green shirt he had on today! The man looks just like a frog, that's what. A self-satisfied frog! I was afraid to shake his hand for fear of getting warts.''

"Frogs don't give warts," Clarice said loudly. "And neither do toads. That's just a superstition."

"Oh!" Mrs. Vickers was so startled, she jumped. It puzzled me that she could hear invisible spirits tiptoe around in corners, but she never seemed able to hear two real people clomping into an empty room. "Why, hello girls, hello. Look, Emmett, it's Flee Jay and her sweet little sister."

"Them!" said Emmett.

"She's not really all that sweet," I wanted to say, but Emmett's complaints drowned out anybody else's words.

"I don't mind your talk about impossible things, Aunt Emma—about creatures that aren't human or stuff like that—when you're talking to those crazies who believe all that hogwash about spirits and mind-reading and who knows what all, but it grinds my gears when you talk that way to business people. Normal people. People like Crandell Teeters."

Mrs. Vickers stood up straighter, but she still hardly reached Emmett's shoulder. She patted her turban. "No need to shout, Emmett. Especially in front of the girls." She turned to us and lowered her voice. "He spouts off like this now and then, but just ignore him. For ten years, I've taken care of this boy, and I know him through and through. He's really just as meek as a lamb."

Then, as though she believed Emmett hadn't been able to hear what she'd just said, even though he stood there frowning at her, she raised her voice again. "Well now, are you girls all set to work? I knew you'd take my job offer. You see? I'm wearing my work clothes. This suit must have shrunk in the wash, though. It seems a mite tight. But my goodness, Clarice. White? Should you wear such fine white clothes for these dirty jobs?''

"Oh, she'll stay clean," I said, and I didn't have a doubt about it. Clarice could fall into a coal pit and come out all neat and tidy.

"Did Mr. Teeters make another offer?" she asked.

"Yes, and I sent him packing again!" Emmett declared. "This building and the land it stands on is worth twice what he says he'll pay—with or without Aunt Emma's ghosts!"

"Spirits," Mrs. Vickers said. "Or entities, dear boy. Ghosts sound too much like children in sheets on Halloween."

"It *all* sounds like Halloween to me!" Emmett said. "Somebody real is behind the problems we've had in here. Somebody real tampered with your iced tea. Twice! Somebody human." He reached into his pocket and pulled out a huge ring clattering with keys. "And these babies are going to prove it!"

"He put padlocks on all the doors last night," Mrs. Vickers said.

"That's right," Emmett triumphantly announced. He turned, and I saw that beneath his scraggly beard he had a nice smile. "I have the only keys, so I am the only one who can open these doors."

Mrs. Vickers nodded. "And last night he made sure everything was in perfect order in each room before he locked it up."

46

"And everything will be in perfect order today too," Emmett announced, heading for the closed doors. "When you lock things up properly, nobody, not even imaginary ghosts, can get inside. See this?" He flung open the door to the kitchen. "Everything exactly as I left it!"

We all trooped over and peered into the room. Sure enough, it looked untouched. The old refrigerator was chugging noisily, but the stove and the counters were silent and uncluttered. No poisoned ice cubes or tea bags were in sight.

"Think we should leave our lunches here?" I asked Clarice.

"Of course, of course," Mrs. Vickers cried. "Right here on the counter. Everything will be all nice and safe there. I packed lunches for me and Emmett too. Now then, all of the cleaning supplies are in the cupboard right over—"

Emmett stopped his aunt's words. "We can tend to that in a minute, Aunt Emma. First I want these kids to check each room so that they can see there's nothing mysterious about this place." He flung out his long arms. "So you agree? This kitchen looks fine?"

"Peachy keen," I said, imitating Dad when he talks like they did in the old days.

And I could have said the same thing for the next two rooms too. They lay before us all empty and bare. Dirty, paint-peeling, but normal.

"You see?" Emmett asked. "You see? No spirts at work here, Aunt Emma. If the doors are locked securely, things stay safe. Things stay exactly the way we left them. Once we clean up these two rooms, they'll be the locker rooms—one for the men, and one for the women. Come on, now, we'll check out this last room. You'll see it's as normal as the other rooms.''

We all trooped to the door marked JUCUZZI. I saw Clarice's eyebrows flicker at the misspelling, but she didn't say anything out loud. In her mind, though, I knew she was plotting for a way to make some changes. Clarice believes we're supposed to treat words with respect.

Emmett stuck a key in the padlock on the door. "Last night I set the hot tub up in here. Got a good buy on a used one, and it seemed to be in great shape. I wanted to be sure the thing worked right before I paid in full, so I filled the tub last night to see that it's okay. Hear that motor? Turns on the heat automatically. The water ought to be nice and warm.''

"Emmett got the machine running in no time at all last night," Mrs. Vickers said proudly. "Even though he said he didn't really know much about hot tubs. I stood behind him when he locked the door. Oh my yes, everything in this room will be in fine shape.''

Just as she finished talking, Emmett threw the door open. Steam burst out in a ghostly mist, and then somebody gasped.

Mrs. Vickers caught her breath. "My stars!''

"Oh gross!" Clarice blurted.

Emmett and I just stared. Warm water was bubbling around all right. But it was a bright scary shade of red. Blood? Was it blood?

"This is impossible!" Emmett shouted. "What's in that water? It was absolutely clear last night!" He held up the key, as though he needed to prove that he still had it. "That door was locked! I'm the only one who had the key, and I know this water was fine last night! This is impossible! Nobody could have snuck inside here last night. Nobody!"

Mrs. Vickers cleared her throat. She took a deep breath. "Nobody human, that is," she whispered.

Impossible Happenings

Clarice ran over and stared into the tub. My skin crawled as she leaned closer, touched, and then even smelled the water. "Looks like red dye," she said, straightening up. "Plain old red dye."

Emmett was beside her in two huge steps. He splashed his hand into the water. "Right! That's what it is, all right." His voice quavered with such relief that I knew his first thought had been that there was blood in that tub too. "Just plain old red dye. Somebody human did this, all right."

But Mrs. Vickers and I didn't share their certainty. She glanced at me and raised her eyebrows. I guess we both had the same questions. Maybe the liquid was only red dye—or maybe it wasn't—but the big question was, how could it have ended up in that hot tub? Who could get in and out of a locked room to put it there?

"It's another warning from the spirits," Mrs. Vickers declared, "just like the warnings with the tea. Surely you have to agree now, Emmett, that I ought to leave. They're trying to show me that I don't belong here."

"Rubbish!" Emmett shook his head. "Somebody *hu-*

man is up to something here. You can be sure of that. I don't know how and I don't know who, but I aim to find out. The one thing I know for sure is that this room was locked up tighter than a drum last night, so we're dealing with somebody pretty clever.''

"Maybe somebody else has a key," Clarice said.

He shook his head. "Nope. I just bought those padlocks, and I have both keys for each lock.''

Clarice studied the ceiling and the walls. "There must be another way to get in here, then. Somebody had to be in here to pour the red dye into the water.''

But there were no windows and no large air vents. Suddenly we were all looking at the closed closet door on the far side of the room. "Could someone have been hiding in there last night when you locked up?'' Clarice asked.

Emmett rubbed his scraggly beard. "I guess so. I mean, I didn't even think to check inside that closet. But if somebody was hiding in there, then how would he get back out of this room again? The door was padlocked on the outside, and I'm the only one with a key.''

"Maybe," I said, and my voice squeaked a little as I spoke, "maybe he's still in there.''

For a second, nobody said anything. Maybe all of us were visualizing a man crouched inside that tiny room waiting to spring out at us. Suddenly I thought I could hear scratching sounds against the closed door. Maybe Emmett thought he heard the same thing. Anyway, he whirled around and marched across the room. He flung open the door.

"Nobody!'' he cried triumphantly as we all stared at

the empty shelves. Then he realized that his triumph meant that we still couldn't explain how a human could have come into a locked room, and his pride evaporated. Even his beard seemed to droop. "This is impossible," he said.

His aunt folded her arms. "Not impossible at all! Emmett, I keep telling you, I'm being warned. This is just another sort of warning and I'm the one who can interpret it. The spirits are my friends. They're trying to tell me that—"

"Now, now, Aunt Emma, I'm not going to listen to that mumble-jumble. I'm not going to let you go. Uncle John wanted us to work this place together. I'll get to the bottom of this somehow. There has to be a logical explanation for what's happening."

Clarice beamed when he used her favorite word, but he sounded more confident than he looked as he crossed over and patted Mrs. Vickers on her shoulder. "You go ahead and start sweeping up in the locker rooms. The girls and I will clean up this mess in here while I do some heavy thinking. We'll get that tub emptied and cleaned. Whoever's trying to sabotage us isn't going to scare us off, and that's all there is to it."

I have to admit it. I didn't like handling that red water. I wasn't altogether sure that it was as harmless as Emmett and Clarice thought. My first impression—that the hot tub was full of blood—kept nagging at me. When I whispered that idea to Clarice, she snorted. "You've watched too many dumb horror shows," she told me.

Maybe so, I told myself. But there *was* something creepy going on in that health club, and even logical Clarice couldn't explain it. I shivered, and I tried to tell myself I was full of goose bumps because I was so wet, but I couldn't fool myself. Ghosts, spirits, or entities—whatever Mrs. Vickers wanted to call them—something seemed to be hovering over my head, making me feel as though snakes were crawling on the back of my neck.

"How does the water in here stay warm?" Clarice asked Emmett when the tub was half emptied.

He went into a long lecture about the machinery, but I turned it off. We didn't have to worry about how the water stayed warm; we needed to be worrying about how the water turned *red*.

As we scoured the red dye out of the tub, I tried to think of ways someone might have broken into that room. The locked door was the biggest puzzle. I thought of some of the mystery books I'd read. "Could there be a secret entrance to this place?" I asked. "Like a tunnel or something that comes up inside one of the closets?"

Emmett sighed. "You think I never thought of that? I checked every inch of this building after the business with Aunt Emma's tea. No, there are no secret doors. No underground tunnels." He swished a sponge around the tub's rim. "But I'll figure this thing out somehow. You'll see, you'll see."

"Or maybe I'll get the answers first," I wanted to say, but I kept quiet. This case was turning out to be harder to solve than I had first thought it might be.

"What do you think?" I whispered to Clarice when Emmett went to get another mop. "How could anyone get in here without a key?"

"Emmett had a key," she whispered back.

"But you don't think that—"

"Shhhhh!" She jabbed my arm. "We'll talk later."

Both of us were busy scrubbing when Emmett walked back into the room. I watched him for a long time, thinking of Clarice's words. He was all flushed and sweaty as he cleaned away red water spots. No, I told myself, he wouldn't have made all that work for himself. Still, though, Clarice usually had some good ideas. Maybe she knew something I didn't know. Hadn't she told me I'd missed a clue when we found Mrs. Vickers flat on the floor? I sighed. It's difficult having a sister who's a genius.

It was nearly time for lunch when we finished in the jacuzzi room. Mrs. Vickers peeked in, her green turban all full of cobwebs, her face streaked with dirt. "I'm ready for food," she said. "Aren't you?"

I smoothed down my sopping shirt. I'd been ready for lunch for more than an hour, actually almost since I had finished breakfast. "I'm glad it's a sunny day. Maybe I can dry off outside. Clarice and I are going to eat in that little park across the street."

Mrs. Vickers smiled. For a few seconds, despite her makeup and turban, she looked almost like my grandmother, all happy and chubby. "Sounds good to me, girls! How about you, Emmett? Want to come join us?"

He shook his head. "Nah. I'll keep working in here, Aunt Emma. I can eat my sandwiches while I wipe down a few walls. The faster we get this place in shape, the quicker we'll be able to open."

"And the quicker you'll be able to get people in shape too!" I said, grinning, but nobody else smiled. It looked as though the Vickers family had a sense of humor as weak as Clarice's.

So just the three of us started for the park.

"Clarice," I whispered as we walked across the street, "I don't think that Emmett—"

"Later," she mumbled. "After lunch."

"Let's sit here, girls," Mrs. Vickers called.

We settled on a bench facing the health club. A nagging thought flickered through my head as I first bit into my sandwich. Hadn't Mrs. Vickers been poisoned by somebody putting something into tea left in that same kitchen? But my hunger pangs were greater than my worry, so I forged ahead. Might as well die happy, I told myself.

It was fun eating while Mrs. Vickers talked. Now that I was used to her strange makeup and clothes, I was beginning to like her a lot. She told Clarice and me all about her life traveling around with the Old Time Circus.

"Oh, it was exciting, girls, really exciting. My John loved show business almost as much as I did. Then Emmett lost his parents. We were lucky enough to have him come join our family, so all three of us traveled around. There wasn't much money, but we didn't care. One time—"

"Do you think he really wants to open the health club?" Clarice interrupted.

Mrs. Vickers blinked at her. "Why of course he does! This will be the perfect way for him to get money for college! He wants to go to college, you know."

"We wondered if he put that red dye in the water himself," I said. Mrs. Vickers stared at me with so much amazement that I quickly added, "I mean, he did have the only key."

"What nonsense!" She shook her head so hard her turban wiggled. "Don't even think such thoughts! Emmett loves the idea of being his own boss in that club. He and my John talked about coming back here one day to open it up together. No, he certainly didn't put dye in that water! And would he put something in my tea to make me faint dead away? No sir! I tell you, girls—and I keep telling him—*I'm* the one the spirits are warning. Once I'm out of the picture, why there won't be any more mysteries. Oh, those spirits are good at giving me messages. One time—"

We sat back and listened to more of her circus stories. I didn't know for sure what Clarice was thinking, but I was sure myself that Emmett wasn't our culprit. But I couldn't go along with the idea of invisible entities fluttering around giving messages either.

Time passed slowly because the park was so quiet. Nobody walked along the streets, and few cars passed. The health club straight across from us looked deserted in the hot sunlight. Now and then, I glanced at it and wondered how Emmett was doing, but for the most part I just plopped and let the rays beam down on my face. Even though I knew I'd just be red and peeling, I liked to think that the hot sun would make me tanned and beautiful. Impossible things were happening all over the place, weren't they? I imagined that I was suddenly skinny too.

Clarice was the first one to jump up. She put her great big mirror back in her purse after checking on her hair (it was perfect, as always) and she nudged my arm. "Hey, aren't we supposed to get back to work?"

I groaned. I might have known that her inner alarm would be the first to start dinging. We gathered up our sandwich wrappers, pop bottles, potato chip bags, and plastic wrappings for alfalfa sprouts. (I'll let you figure out who used what.) Then we went back across the street.

The health club smelled like cleaning supplies when we walked through the door. After the glare of the sun, it was hard to see anything.

"Is that you guys?" Emmett called from a back room.

I was blinking my eyes to get a better focus when he walked toward us. "Nearly have those kitchen walls done," he said. "You can get a lot done when nobody bothers you. We'll be able to start painting when we—"

"What's that?" Mrs. Vickers asked. She was pointing to a black paper lying on the corner of the long desk.

Emmett stared. "What? Well, I sure don't know. I didn't put anything on that desk, and I didn't hear anybody else put anything there. Nobody else even came in here!"

Clarice was the first one to grab it. Her mouth dropped open as she picked up the paper, and then she turned it around for all of us to see. White ink had been used to form letters that twined around like snakes on the black surface. And the message was written inside the hood of a huge, hissing cobra snake. The words had been written by an unsteady hand, fingers that seemed to be writing from a distance

WE ARE WARNING YOU BOTH— ### GET OUT, GET OUT, GET OUT!!!!

And even though I was only reading the words to myself in my own mind, I thought I heard them echoing over and over throughout the dim, silent room. Now it looked as though those mysterious "spirits" were after Emmett as well as Mrs. Vickers.

Clues Are
Where You Find Them

I can hardly remember what we did for the rest of the afternoon. We swept and cleaned for a few more hours, but my mind was so busy thinking about everything that had happened that I hardly noticed what wall I was washing or what floor I was sweeping. I kept seeing that snake in my mind. Did these weird "spirits" that Mrs. Vickers talked about send snakes to carry out their threats? What if I moved some old junk from a closet and a cobra jumped out at me?

"I just can't understand it," Mrs. Vickers whispered to Clarice and me more than once. "I thought I knew everything the spirits could do, but that last warning, why . . ."

Emmett, too, seemed really shook up about the mysterious note, maybe because he had been in the health club when it arrived. He took it as a personal insult that the warning had appeared while he was there. "I never heard a thing," he kept saying. "But I was way back in the kitchen. The back door there is still bolted. Are you sure you didn't see somebody come in or out of that front door?"

"Nobody told us to watch," Clarice told him. I could

see that she was annoyed. Old Eagle Eyes Clarice would have noticed a gnat winging through that door if she'd set her mind to watching it, but none of us had guessed that it would be important. She looked at Emmett again. "But I don't think so. I don't think anybody at all walked on the street out in front."

"She's right," I said. "I was sunning, but I almost always had my eyes open. And I was facing the street. Nobody walked in front of the health club building, Emmett. Nobody walked along that street."

"But that's impossible!" he burst out, looking angry and frustrated. I guess we all felt the same way. If things can't be explained, at first they make you feel puzzled—but then they can make you feel mad. I wondered all over again if Emmett was the guilty one. He had been all alone when the mysterious message arrived, I told myself. But then I argued back—he'd been just as puzzled as the rest of us, and I didn't think he had just been acting. And I sure couldn't think of any reason why he'd want to do such crazy things!

My mind was reeling and my body was aching when we got ready to leave at the end of the day. My fingers looked as wrinkled as prunes because my hands had been in water so much. "Some health club," I mumbled to Clarice, as I put away the brooms. "I've never felt so *un*healthy."

"You've been good workers, good workers," Mrs. Vickers chirped as she joined us in the kitchen. She looked tired and discouraged, but she was still trying to be cheerful. Her turban was slightly tipped, so she righted it and patted strands of gray hair up under it. "I'm just sorry that these terrible things are going on, that's what. That note today, why, it was like a bolt from the blue! I thought I knew my spirits, but—''

''Could I do an experiment in here, Mrs. Vickers?'' Clarice asked. She took her purse out of the closet. ''I was thinking that I would like to leave something in this room that belongs to me.'' She pulled out her mirror. Actually, her carrying it around was a huge waste of energy because her hair never gets mussed, but the mirror was in the shape of a heart with a red plastic rim, so I guess it was pretty even if it didn't serve much purpose.

Clarice put it on the counter by the sink. ''The note warned both of you away. I wonder what might happen if I leave something of mine in this locked room. Will some message warn me away too?''

''Go ahead and leave anything you want in here,'' Emmett said. He pushed back his straggly hair and pulled his keys out of his pocket. ''I'll lock this room. Nobody ought to be able to get inside, but after all this weird stuff—'' He waved his hand and then shrugged. ''Well, I'll tell you, kid, I just plain don't know *what* might happen,'' he added as he ushered us to the door.

Looking back, I squinted my eyes and tried to scrutinize every inch of the room, exactly the way a real detective would. Finally, I was satisfied. The room was empty. Clarice's mirror was the only thing lying on the counter.

''One more thing,'' Clarice said. She opened her purse again and yanked out a rubber band. ''I saw this on a television show once. Let me put this in the crack as you shut the door. When we open the door tomorrow, we'll look for the rubber band to fall to the floor. If the door hasn't been opened during the night, it has to fall."

I had to give the kid credit. It was a great idea. "Ghosts wouldn't need to open the door," I said, "so if the rubber band doesn't fall when we open the door, that will mean somebody human has gotten in and out of here. Ghosts could go right through the door. Couldn't they?" Mrs. Vickers frowned, and so I quickly added, "I mean 'spirits.' "

"It's a fine experiment," she said, nodding. She turned to Emmett. "Didn't I tell you that I had a good feeling about these two girls? My vibrations are never wrong. They're going to help us in lots of ways."

As he locked the door, Emmett just grunted. He looked almost as tired as I felt.

"Now don't open this door until we're all here together in the morning, Emmett," Clarice told him. "Then we'll all be witnesses to see whether that rubber band is still in place."

When we were back outside by our bikes, I sighed. "I don't know if I can even pedal this bike home. I feel like I was caught in a cement mixer."

Clarice hopped on her bike. "I guess that means that you don't want to go with me to Hardwick's Department Store."

If my teeth hadn't been wired in place, I might have dropped them. "What? Why in the world do you want to go over there?"

She shrugged. "I want to check on something."

"Well, I want a hot shower, a cold glass of lemonade, and a soft chair," I told her. "Right in that order."

Clarice started moving south. "Okay. I'll go over to Main

63

Street this way then. I'll be home before Mom and Dad are." I stared after her for just a moment, wondering how she had so much energy. Maybe the greatest mystery of my life will be trying to figure out how and why my sister does what she does.

My legs and arms ached as I pedaled, but the thought of that hot shower kept me going. I hardly paid any attention to poor old Ginger as she barked a welcome to me when I came in the back door. But I did stop long enough to peek carefully into the bathroom before I stepped in. If there had been a red ring around that tub, I might have changed my plans. When I was a little kid, I often took a shower with the hose in the backyard, and rather than face another red tub, I was ready to hop into a bathing suit and shower outside again.

As soon as I was clean and dressed, I hurried to the kitchen to get that glass of lemonade. There was a plate of cookies on the counter, so I grabbed a few of them too. I suddenly thought of my friend, Tara. Her little sister spits on all the cookies in the house, so she's the only one who'll eat them. Clarice is weird, but not *that* weird, I told myself, settling down with my snack. Maybe I was lucky that she preferred alfalfa sprouts to cookies. She could spit on all the sprouts she wanted, and it wouldn't bother me a bit. But of course I know Clarice wouldn't be caught dead spitting on anything at all.

As I sat there, I remembered how she said she'd seen a clue about Mrs. Vickers's tea. I looked at my huge glass of lemonade and wondered what Clarice had seen in that health club that had been invisible to me. "Plain as can be to anybody who looks," she had told me.

The only thing that was plain about *my* glass was that it was empty. Oh, it had plenty of ice cubes, all right, but I needed more lemonade. I hurried over to the refrigerator and poured more.

Maybe my sudden movement scared Ginger. She's always been a bit hyper. Anyway, I don't know what possessed her, but she jumped up against me at that same moment, and I dropped the glass. Lemonade and ice cubes went splishing and splattering all over the kitchen carpet. Grumbling, I reached for a cloth. Mom would be home in minutes—that carpet would have to be cleaned up by the time she walked into the kitchen.

When I was down on my knees, I realized that our carpet was almost the same color as the brown carpet at the health club. Ours was a whole lot newer, but for a second or two I almost felt as though I was back there looking at the stains made by the tea on the morning we'd first met Mrs. Vickers. I stared at the huge wet blob spreading out in front of me, the ice cubes scattered far beyond it.

And then, suddenly, I saw it. I saw the clue that Clarice had been talking about. This stain didn't look at all like the tea stain there. And, as I remembered Clarice feeling the carpet, I knew this stain didn't feel like that one either.

"Where were the ice cube stains?" I asked Ginger. "Mrs. Vickers said there were ice cubes in her tea. She said she had just put them in there before she dropped the glass. But ice cubes bounce on carpets! See?"

I inched forward on my knees and gathered up the cubes—they were scattered far ahead of the rest of the spill. "How come there weren't any stains or wet spots from where the ice cubes melted on the carpet ahead of Mrs. Vickers's big spill?''

Ginger stared at me, blinking and thinking, maybe imitating my face exactly.

But neither one of us could come up with an answer.

Thoughts of Murder

Mom came in just as I finished cleaning the carpet, and Clarice walked in five minutes after that. With all the commotion of getting dinner, I couldn't talk to her alone. My discovery was thundering in my head like a bowling ball in the gutter.

"Ice cubes bounce," I finally managed to hiss as we were setting the table.

She whirled around in surprise, and then she grinned and nodded. "So you finally figured it out. Yeah, that's the clue I was talking about!"

"So why did Mrs. Vickers mention ice cubes?" I asked. "She must have been lying about having ice cubes in her glass. Do you think she was only faking about fainting too?"

"Well, I think—" Clarice's words were cut off by the back door opening. Dad hurried inside, rubbing his hands together and beaming. "So can I quit my job while you two support me in the future? How was the first day of work, girls?"

Clarice and I looked at each other again, not even sure

how to begin. How can you explain an elephant when the only animal somebody knows is a guinea pig?

"I'll bet you're both tired," Dad went on, so then we were able to talk about aching muscles and we didn't have to mention any of the weird stuff that had happened.

When we were almost through with dinner, Mom nodded toward the calendar. "I hope you won't be too tired at Wilson's birthday party tonight, Clarice."

Both of us groaned. I groaned because that meant Clarice and I wouldn't be alone to talk, and she groaned because she can't stand Wilson Galinski. He's the son of Mom's boss, and he's in the same grade as Clarice. He looks okay to me, but she says he's a throwback to Neanderthal Man.

"Guess I did forget," she said.

Mom frowned. "Honestly, Clarice! You can remember a telephone number you dialed only once six months ago, but you can't remember a simple date on the calendar! You know how much Wilson likes you. Pete tells me he's been looking forward to seeing you for weeks now."

"No harm done," Dad said. "You remembered it, Linda. You can drive Clarice to the party on your way to that league meeting tonight."

"But I didn't get Wilson a present," Clarice said.

"I was afraid you hadn't thought about a gift," Mom said, "so I stopped and bought him something at lunch today. His dad says he's into military stuff now, so I bought him a remote-controlled tank."

I nearly spluttered out the milk I was drinking. Imagining

nerdy Wilson Galinski driving a tank was almost as laughable as imagining Michael Jackson dancing a polka.

Clarice threw a desperate look at me. "But tonight I was going to—"

"Well now, Clarice—" Mom put down her fork and picked up the rhythm of her words. Clarice was going to get a familiar lecture about how she had to socialize more with her friends and stop being so wrapped up in her own projects. I let the words bounce off my ears. Both Clarice and I had heard them all before. Mom wants us to taste all of life, she keeps telling us.

So maybe it's her fault that I'm a little chubby. She wanted me to taste a lot.

We never had a chance to say anything more at the table. "We'll talk later," Clarice whispered to me as Mom whisked her out the door half an hour later.

As I cleared the dishes, I tried to imagine what Clarice might tell me. I wondered if she thought Mrs. Vickers might be lying about everything—maybe even just pretending that she was unconscious when we first met her. I couldn't see any reason for her to do that, though. And it didn't seem possible that she could have done the other things. She didn't have a key to get into the room with the hot tub, and we had been with her when that note had been delivered. Did Emmett do those things? Once again my fingers were puckered from being in water as I did all the dishes, and once again my head was whirling with questions as I thought about that health club.

Questions always make me hungry. As soon as I had the kitchen gleaming, I popped up a big bowl of popcorn for me and Dad. I added butter and syrup and brown sugar to it too. Calories increase brain power some- times.

They didn't seem to help me that night, though. I was nearly itching with frustration when Clarice got home. I could see right away that she was in a rotten mood. While I'd been Snow White cleaning up that kitchen, she'd turned into Grumpy.

"It was the dumbest party I've ever been to," she complained as we went upstairs to our rooms. "They played 'Spin the Bottle.' The one who spins gets to kiss the person it points to. Can you believe it? Wilson kissed me! Oh yuck! Double yuck! Quadruple yuc—"

I stopped her before she could go any further. With a mathematical wizard like Clarice, the yucks could have gone on into infinity. I nudged her and joked, "Why didn't you whip the disinfectant out of your purse and spray him?"

She looked absolutely serious. "I never thought of that."

"Well, it's a good thing!" I said. "Mom might have lost her job if you'd tried a trick like that. Good grief, I was only kidding, Clarice. Anyway, that's enough about that stupid birthday party. Since ice cubes bounce, we know Mrs. Vickers lied about having them in that glass. Right?"

We stopped in front of my bedroom door. Clarice pulled at the strap on her purse. "Sure looks that way, Flee Jay. There wasn't any dampness at all on that carpet beyond the first spill. I felt it all. You should have done that too. If you're going to be a good detective, you ought to be more careful. You hardly even looked at that carpet, and yet it gave us our first clue. You don't really investigate things enough you know. You—"

"Oh, chill out, Clarice! Let's not talk about me and my minor faults! Let's talk about Mrs. Vickers. Why would she lie? And what about all the other crazy things going on in that health club? Do you think Mrs. Vickers somehow did those things too? Do you think Emmett did them?"

"I don't know. But I'm going to get some answers tomorrow."

I jerked up straighter. "You are? How?"

She moved down the hall toward her bedroom. "You wouldn't go to Hardwick's with me today, so you don't deserve to know. That's where I found another big clue."

I took a few steps down the hall. "Well now, Clarice—" I knew I sounded exactly like Mom, but I didn't care. "I didn't know that Hardwick's Department Store had anything to do with solving this mystery! You never said anything about any clues! I thought you were just going there to look at their new computers or their billing system or some other dumb thing. What'd you find out that would help us with the case?"

"Plenty!" Clarice answered as she ducked inside her room.

I was right behind her. "But *I'm* the detective! If you found out something important, you'd better tell me!"

Clarice jerked the door almost tight, then she peeked out at me through the crack. "Nanny, nanny, boo, boo. You can't do what I do!'' The door slammed shut on her last word.

"You're a rat!'' I muttered against it. My thoughts of our health club mystery briefly turned to thoughts of murder, and for a few seconds I felt like strangling Clarice. But I knew I'd never be able to get away with it. Mom and Dad would have known right away that I did it. Who else would have such a good motive?

I went to bed wondering why I couldn't have been born an only child.

Strange Confession

The next morning I tried to get Clarice to tell me more about how she was going to get some answers, but she just shrugged, nibbled on her bran muffin, and dabbed her face with her napkin. "It's not for sure, Flee Jay," she said. "I mean I don't know how this whole thing is going to turn out, so I can't tell you anything until we get to the health club. If I'm wrong, you'll never know just how far off the truth I really was. I hate it when I make a mistake."

"And the sun rises every morning," I wanted to say, but instead I took another bite of peanut butter toast. "Does it have anything to do with that rubber band you left in the crack of the door of that kitchen?" I finally asked.

"Maybe." She reached for a second napkin. Nobody, but nobody, uses as many napkins as my sister.

"Shall we ask Mrs. Vickers about those ice cubes?"

Her hand fell, and I saw that I'd hit a sore point. "Don't do that, Flee Jay! You'd spoil it."

"Spoil what?"

But I might as well have been asking questions of a statue. We rode all the way to the health club without speaking. I was pretty sure Clarice's answers revolved around Mrs.

Vickers and those ice cubes, though. It made me mad that I was the detective, but my sister seemed to be doing more with the case than I was. The more I thought about it, the harder I pedaled, so I guess my anger served a good purpose. We made it to the health club in record time.

Emmett and Mrs. Vickers were unlocking the front door when we pulled our bikes up in front. Emmett looked as though he was wearing the same jeans and shirt he had worn the day before, but Mrs. Vickers was wearing completely different clothes. Now she was back to being the fortune-telling lady with the "eyes" that could see all. It didn't look as though she planned to help clean today. Her outfit was red, with a gold design, and her turban was red too. She wore the same belled necklace she had worn before.

I had a strange feeling as I looked at her. On the one hand she was an eerie lady with an air of mystery about her, and on the other hand she was an elderly woman who seemed a lot like my grandmother. I wondered who the "real" Emma Vickers was. She had lied about those ice cubes, so maybe she had lied about other things too. But it didn't seem possible that she had been able to get into a locked room—had been able to leave a note when she had been with me and Clarice throughout the whole noon hour. Did she somehow have real magic powers?

Emmett yanked on the door. His straggly hair bounced around as he pulled on the handle. "This darn key is stuck! Well, I guess this proves that getting into this club is not easy."

"You think my mirror is okay?" Clarice asked.

Mrs. Vickers caught her breath. "Oh my, I hope so! But

74

after yesterday, I just don't know. Spirits do have incredible powers, you know, and they—''

"At least it will be cleaner inside than it was yesterday," I blurted, not wanting to make any of us more nervous about those "spirits" than we already were. "We worked hard enough yesterday to be sure of that."

Mrs. Vickers looked down at her robe. "And I'll be doing just as much washing up today as I did yesterday," she told me, and once again I worried that she had read my mind. "It's just that I didn't feel like myself when I was wearing that foolish sweat suit. I feel more like myself wearing something like this." She lifted a fold of her long skirt. "These robes are completely washable, so I decided to go ahead and wear one. They're polyester, you know."

I almost giggled out loud. Somehow it struck me funny that a woman who talked about unseen spirits and supernatural powers would ever worry about something as ordinary as washable clothes. I tried to imagine Mrs. Vickers in a soap commercial on TV. "Yes, friends," she might say, "with Whammo suds, you'll surely have good fortune. You can get your clothes so clean that the dirt won't have a ghost of a chance. Your spirits will be lifted with—''

"There!" Emmett cried, cutting off my mental picture, and the door swung open. The huge room lay empty and quiet in front of us. There was no warning note on the desk (that was the first place I looked) and there was no sign that anybody had been inside since we had left.

"Looks as though everything is fine," Emmett said, his voice shaking with relief. "Sure am glad about that! For a while I was beginning to—''

Clarice hurried across the room to the kitchen door.

"Let's look to see if that rubber band is right where we left it. It ought to fall down unless that door was opened by somebody else before we got here."

I bolted right after her. If there was another big clue to what was happening, then this time I was going to be right there the minute she saw it.

Emmett struggled with this lock too, and I could see that he was nervous. When he finally pushed the door open, we all stumbled inside. He and Mrs. Vickers and I practically bumped heads as we all bent to see whether a rubber band would fall to the ground.

"It just fell!" I shouted, grabbing it.

"So nobody got in!" Emmett declared, all triumphant.

"But look!" Clarice had run to the counter, and now she held up her mirror. It was broken in two, shattered right down the middle of the heart. "Somebody got in here and broke this," she said, sounding like Baby Bear in the old fairy tale.

Mrs. Vickers sagged against the counter. "That's impossible," she mumbled.

"It can't be!" Emmett shouted. His face was all tight and scared looking. "Nobody opened this door. Nobody opened that back door. Look—it's still bolted on the inside. This whole thing is impossible. Nobody could have gotten in here to break that mirror because that rubber band was still in place!"

"Unless the person who opened the door simply put the rubber band back in place when he closed it up again," Clarice said, staring at him.

"But we're the only ones who knew that it was there,"

Emmett told her, "and none of us would do a silly thing like that! Right, Aunt Emma?"

Mrs. Vickers was gasping. She was pale under her thick makeup, and she was trembling.

He bent over her. "Are you all right, Aunt Emma?"

"I guess I should have brought my tonic, dear." She tried to stand straighter, but she was still shaking and her voice was all quavery. "I left it home in the bathroom medicine chest. I think it would calm me a bit. Could you get it, dear? Could you get it?"

Emmett was running for the door before she finished. "I'll be right back!" he shouted.

As soon as he was gone, she stood up, her necklace bells tinkling. "Oh girls," she whispered. "I think I've really unleashed a terrible power. I must have done something horribly wrong." She blinked and started to say more, but Clarice cut off her words.

"Twice you made up the story about the tea. Once with Emmett and once with us. You only pretended to be unconscious on the floor when we found you. There wasn't any poison in your tea. There weren't even any ice cubes."

Mrs. Vickers's mouth fell open. "But how did you—"

"And you put red dye in the filtering mechanism of that hot tub," Clarice went on. "You did it the night before you and Emmett left. The dye was in a plastic bag that dissolved in water. When the heating element automatically went on late in the night, the water circulated through that filtering system, the plastic melted, and the dye turned the water red."

Now it was my turn to gasp.

"I went over to Hardwick's Department Store and looked

at a hot tub just like the one here," Clarice told me. "Once I saw how the water circulated inside that filter every eight hours, I knew exactly how a 'spirit' could turn the water red."

"Oh girls!" Mrs. Vickers clasped her hands to her chest. "You must think I'm a terrible person, trying to fool everyone, trying to scare everyone that way. But I have a good reason, girls, I have a good reason." She leaned closer. "You see, I want Emmett to have this club all on his own. My John left it to both of us, so I know Emmett feels obligated to share with me. But I don't like this business and never much liked it."

"Then why don't you just leave?" I asked.

"But don't you see? It's not that simple! Emmett feels he owes it to John to work with me here. And he thinks that he needs to take care of me. He's such a dear, dear boy. I don't have the heart to tell him I don't want to stay here with him. He's said again and again if I don't stay with him, then he wouldn't feel right about staying here and making money on his own. He says he's sure that's what his Uncle John would want. I thought if the spirits warned me off, then Emmett would be willing to let me go and try it on his own. How could he go against the will of unseen spirits?"

She moved closer to us. "I didn't want him to suspect that I was eager to leave, you see. But I never dreamed that you girls would find me on the floor like that! I thought Emmett would! I feel terrible that I frightened you so!"

I thought of all the things I'd seen Emmett do and say the past few days. "Maybe Emmett doesn't really want to run this club either," I said.

Mrs. Vickers sighed. "But he needs the money it could bring. If Emmett could just run this place for a few years, he'd have enough for college. Then he could get someone else to take over. It's college that he really wants."

"Then selling this place would be best for both of you," Clarice said.

"Maybe. Maybe so." Mrs. Vickers shook her head. "But the only one making an offer is that awful Crandell Teeters. And his offer was hardly worth looking at." She sighed again. "Oh, I guess I must look like a fool. But my plans made sense when I first thought of them. With me out of the way, I thought Emmett could do a far better job here. And the money I earned at the circus could help him a bit too."

"So you pretended that someone was tampering with your tea," I said. "You turned that hot tub water red. You left that 'warning' note, and you broke Clarice's mirror."

"No!" She grabbed my arm. She frantically looked at Clarice. "That's what I mean about unleashing some sort of terrible power in here. I didn't leave that note! Truly I didn't! I don't know how that was done. And I didn't break the mirror! I don't know how that was done either!" She flung her hands to her chest, and her necklace bells clattered together again. "I've talked about the powers of spirits for years, but I never really believed in most of what I said. It was all show, all entertainment for people. But now I don't know, girls. I just don't know! I swear I didn't have anything to do with that warning note. I swear I didn't have anything to do with that broken mirror."

"Maybe Emmett did those things," I said. But I didn't really believe my own words. Emmett Vickers could never

80

have pretended his surprise—and fear—when he saw that Clarice's mirror had been broken.

"Oh no," Mrs. Vickers whispered. "I'm absolutely certain Emmett had nothing to do with any of these tricks. Nobody human could have done those things. That's why I'm so worried. I'll tell you something, girls. I'm really frightened now."

Another Confession

I felt scared to death that moment too. As foolish as it sounds, I have to admit it. For a second it felt as though the air in that room was rushing in to suffocate me, that Mrs. Vickers's fear was pulsating all around us.

Clarice moved closer to Mrs. Vickers. "You really didn't write that note?"

"Or break the mirror either! Oh, girls, could I have unleashed some *real* power with all of my tricks all these years? My act has really just been a show, you know, with some lucky guesses. Fortune-telling is just show business, like movies or stage plays. Everybody knows that. People just like to imagine that some of us have special powers, so fortune-tellers create that illusion. I never harmed anyone. People were entertained, that's all. They all knew my powers were only pretend. I've only been like an actress, you see, and I talked and dressed the part. That's why I only feel comfortable dressed in these clothes."

She gestured at her robe, then she looked back up at me. "But perhaps I've touched on something supernatural with all of my pretense. Maybe there *are* spirits of some sort. and I've angered them. Could it be? Could it be?" She blinked as she gazed around the room. "It has to be supernatural. Who else could have done these impossible things?"

As if in answer, the front door banged. "I'm back!" Emmett shouted.

Clarice and I glanced at each other, but Mrs. Vickers faced the door. "I'm going to tell Emmett the whole story. Maybe he'll understand and forgive me if I tell him the truth."

It took her a long time to do it. Clarice and I wanted to leave, but we were cornered there in the kitchen while Emmett stood in the doorway listening to his aunt. It was embarrassing to watch his face turn from interest to confusion to anger while she told him how she'd fooled him with the tea and the red water.

"But for pete's sake, Aunt Emma!" he kept interrupting. "You didn't have to do that! You could have talked to me. We could have worked things out. You didn't have to pull all those tricks!"

"Well, I didn't want to hurt you, and I thought my plan would solve everything," she explained. "I never guessed— I never dreamed—that I would end up making even more trouble for everyone. I'm sorry that I frightened you and the girls. I acted foolishly, Emmett. I can see that now. It would have been far better just to come right out and talk to you. It's always better to tell the truth, I guess."

"So will you tell the truth now too?" I burst out. I looked at Emmett. "Did you write that warning note and break Clarice's mirror?"

"Me!" Emmett's beard wiggled. His hair nearly straightened in surprise. "Me? Why would I do things as crazy as

83

that? No! Running a health club is not my idea of a great life, but I know I need money for college. Uncle John thought we should work here together. I knew Aunt Emma wasn't gung-ho for the idea, but I thought she felt she had to leave for *my* sake. I never guessed she really didn't want to be here at all. She didn't have to play those tricks to make me understand. And I sure never thought of playing any tricks on her!''

''You really didn't write that note?'' Clarice asked. ''You didn't leave it out there on the desk?''

He glared at her. ''I sure as heck didn't! I've told you from the beginning I don't believe in 'spirits.' Why would I pretend to be one?''

''And you didn't break that mirror?'' I asked.

''I never even touched that mirror!''

''I broke the mirror,'' Clarice said quietly.

All three of us whirled around to stare at her. She flushed, and smoothed back her hair. ''I thought I needed to do something incredible so that you all could see that it doesn't take 'spirits' to do something impossible,'' she explained. ''I thought that would be a way to get everybody to tell the truth.'' She paused. ''And my idea worked, didn't it?''

Mrs. Vickers's face was wrinkled in confusion. ''You broke your own mirror?''

''But how'd you do it?'' I blurted. ''You were home in bed all night. The outside door here was locked and this kitchen door was locked.''

''And I had the only keys!'' Emmett cried. ''How'd you get inside here to break that mirror? How could you get in and out again?''

Clarice folded her arms. She grinned. "There are lots of ways to make people think you came in and out of a locked room. Mrs. Vickers, you just told us about the illusions you use in your fortune-telling. People let themselves be fooled. That's how magicians work. They use props so that they can fool people into believing in magic. I used a prop for my trick too."

I glared at her, feeling more and more angry that she hadn't shared her plans with me. "What prop?"

"The rubber band in the door crack."

"But that wasn't an illusion. It was really there. It fell to the floor when we opened that door. I saw it fall."

"Yes, and you and Emmett and Mrs. Vickers all bent to get it," Clarice said. "Remember? That's all the three of you were thinking about when we came through the doorway. So I ran right over to the mirror and broke it while you all were shouting about the rubber band falling. Nobody saw or heard me. By the time you looked at me, the mirror was already broken. I just held it up and you all thought it had been broken during the night."

"Wow!" Emmett looked more impressed than angry. "That was some trick! I'll have to remember that one. Sure fooled me!"

"Better even than my red dye," Mrs. Vickers said, beaming. "I could use you in my act, Clarice. You know as much about doing the impossible as I do."

"That's because she *is* impossible!" I muttered. "How come you couldn't have told me your plan?"

"Because I wasn't one hundred percent sure it would work. And besides, you're a terrible actress, Flee Jay. You probably would have watched me instead of reaching for that rubber band and my whole plan might have—"

"Well, you still could have told me. You—"

"So how'd you deliver that warning letter without anybody seeing?" Emmett asked, all eager and interested.

Clarice wilted. "I didn't."

Mrs. Vickers blinked. "You didn't? Well, you all know that I didn't!"

"I didn't do it either," Emmett cried.

"Then who did?" Clarice asked.

"Not me!" I said as everybody turned to look at me. "I never tried to trick anybody at all!"

Emmett heaved a sigh. "So are we back to the 'spirits' again then?"

It seemed that we were. No matter how much we talked, we couldn't figure out who could have written and delivered that note.

"Well, guess we'll never know the answer to that one," Emmett finally declared. "But I sure feel better about the rest of all this far-out stuff. Let's make some plans, Aunt Emma. Don't ever think you can't tell me how you really feel about things."

"And you can be sure I won't be leaving until I've helped you get things in order around here first," Mrs. Vickers said. "John would have wanted me to do that. I can—"

Clarice and I left them talking in the kitchen while we washed walls in the main room. I was still bummed at her for not telling me all her plan, so I took my own bucket and stayed on my own side of the room. Clarice thought she was smart, but the whole case wasn't solved yet, I kept telling myself. Maybe I could still solve the mystery of who wrote that warning note.

I could only hope that nothing big would happen while I was at the dentist's. It's hard to be a detective when you're young. Instead of straightening out suspects, sometimes you have to spend your time straightening out your teeth.

Thank You, Ms. Attila the Hun

"I'll be back just as quick as I can," I told Clarice and Mrs. Vickers as soon as I had gobbled down my potato chips and sandwiches at lunch time. We had gone back to the small park to eat, and they were both sitting on the bench facing the health club. Nobody had said anything about watching that front door, but I think all three of us had eaten with one eye on our lunch and the other on that sidewalk. Like me, I guess Mrs. Vickers and Clarice weren't going to let a single person walk by without our noticing who and why and how.

But so far only a few people had passed on that sidewalk, and nobody had even paused in front of the health club.

"Now don't rush, dear," Mrs. Vickers said. "We can manage here."

"And don't forget to brush your teeth first," Clarice called after me as I hurried back across the street. "Remember Ms. Attila the Hun and her jackhammer!"

She knew she didn't need to remind me. Before I go to the dentist I brush and clean my teeth like a wild woman. It's a wonder I don't strangle myself with dental floss as I whip it in and out of my mouth. The wires on my teeth glisten and gleam when I'm done. I do it because of Ms. Attila the Hun. When she looks into my mouth, I want it to be as clean as I can get it.

Of course Dr. Hertzog's nurse isn't really named Ms. Attila the Hun, but she always goes at her job with such "joyous savage frenzy" (that's what my dad says) that our whole family calls her that. She loves grabbing up her metal picks and gouging off any speck she finds on a tooth. Dad says she did her training with a jackhammer on the streets of New York. He may be closer to the truth than he thinks.

I had brought along my brush and toothpaste, and I was just putting them back into my purse when Emmett came into the kitchen. "That larger locker room is all ready for the paint now," he said. Sighing, he stuck his bucket under the faucet. "But the more I get done, the more I see I haven't done."

He looked as tired and droopy as ice cream cones on the Fourth of July. "Too bad you can't sell this place," I told him.

"You said it." Shrugging, he reached for more soap. "But who'd want to buy a building in this neighborhood? Nothing is going on in this part of town, so nobody wants to buy anything around here. That Teeters fellow is the only one interested and his offer was a joke. It's not just the neighborhood—the building itself is in pretty bad shape. The roof needs to be repaired and the walls aren't insulated. The place is completely run down. We're stuck with it, and we can turn it into a decent enough health club, but nobody would want to buy it. Crandell Teeters knows that."

"So why does he want the building?"

Emmett shrugged. "Beats me."

"If this place is so worthless, I wonder why that note was written," I said. "Who would care that you're here?"

Emmett turned the water on full blast. As it went splashing into his bucket, he frowned. "If I could meet the person—or 'spirit,' as Aunt Emma calls it—who wrote that note, I'd be tempted to hand over the deed and say 'you're welcome to it, fella. If you want this place that badly, you can have it.' "

"But isn't it weird, Emmett? I mean, nobody can still figure out how that note got here."

"Maybe we'll *never* figure it out." Emmett sloshed his bucket of soapy water out from under the faucet and headed back toward the second locker room.

After working inside all morning, I was glad to get back out into the sunshine again. My brain and my body worked so hard that it only took me twenty minutes to get to Dr. Hertzog's office. The results of all my brain work weren't that obvious. I still didn't have any new ideas about that warning note.

There were two women and a little kid sitting in the waiting room. I plopped down by a pile of ancient magazines. I was almost sure they were the same magazines that had been there ever since I started going to the dentist eight years before, but I picked one up, brushed off the dust, and started flipping through. The little kid was blowing bubbles with some green bubble gum while the women talked. I hoped, for his sake, that it was sugarless gum and that Ms. Attila the Hun wouldn't see him. She doesn't approve of anything in the mouth unless it's tasteless, textureless, and nourishing, in that order.

"Yes, Martin says that new mall is going to be terrific,

Wilma," one of the women was whispering. "Grand Channel has needed some discount stores for a long time. Of course we never dreamed that his agency would get all this business from it, but—"

I wasn't really trying to eavesdrop, but any conversation was more interesting than another article about how bees make honey—and this conversation was about a new mall. The only things I like more than malls are potato chips and boys. One is full of calories and the other doesn't know I'm alive, so malls are pretty high on my Interest List. I stared at my magazine and listened.

"This is all still very hush-hush, you know, but as soon as all the contracts are signed, they'll make the big announcement."

"I wish George worked in real estate. You get all the good scoop, Lenore."

"Well, real estate isn't always that interesting, I can tell you. And it's risky too, Wilma. When Martin found out he was supposed to sell that slummy property over on Watson Avenue, we were sure his career was over. Who'd be interested in buying there? We never dreamed that's where that Chicago group planned to build a discount mall. Martin says they've been quietly buying up the property in that area for nearly a year. They say with all the resort trade we have here in the summer, a big discount mall is sure to be a huge success. They were mighty glad to work with Martin on the lots he had. And some of the group are trying to deal with the owners themselves. Why, they need all kinds of land just for parking lots, you know."

A light bulb must have sprung up over my head just the way ideas are shown in comic books. Watson Avenue.

Slummy land. Parking lots. Wasn't most of the area around The Fit and Trim Health Club either deserted or being torn down? Maybe the new mall would be close to Watson Avenue and Dowland Street, where the health club was.

My brain was spinning. Wasn't Crandell Teeters from Chicago? Maybe he knew about the plans. Couldn't the health club be part of the land that could be used for stores or parking lots? And wouldn't Mr. Teeters want to get it as cheaply as possible?

Suddenly I recalled the argument Mrs. Vickers and Emmett had had yesterday morning. Emmett had been mad because she had told Crandell Teeters that mysterious spirits were warning her away from the club. She had really sent those warnings to herself, but Mr. Teeters wouldn't know that. Maybe he thought he'd take advantage of a superstitious old woman and add another "voice" to the clamor she thought she was hearing. The warning note had arrived that very afternoon, hadn't it? Instantly I was convinced that somehow Crandell Teeters was behind that mysterious note. He had probably thought that—

"Felice Jennifer!" The words finally reached my brain. Ms. Attila the Hun was ready for me, but that was all right. I jumped up and beamed my glittering braces at her. Thanks to my appointment with her, I was sure I knew the "who" and "why" of that mysterious note. Now all I had to do was find out the "how."

Fabulous Girl Detective
on the Job

My bike tires went faster than the wheels in the cages of frustrated hamsters at the pet shop as I pedaled back to the Fit and Trim Health Club.

"Any more notes?" I shouted, hurrying in the front door. After the bright sun outside, the room seemed dark and blurry. I blinked in the dim light. Except for a chair standing off to my left, the room was still empty. Following the sound of necklace bells, I saw Mrs. Vickers behind the big desk. By then my eyes had adjusted to the gloom and I saw that Clarice was against the far wall, washing window sills with a huge sponge. Emmett called hello from one of the back rooms.

"No, no more notes," Mrs. Vickers said, looking up from her piles of information sheets. "Clarice and I checked when we came back from lunch. And we've both been right out here in the hour since then."

"You didn't miss a thing, Flee Jay," Clarice said. "The mystery of the weird warning is still not solved."

I whirled around to grin at her. "Well, *part* of it is solved! I think I know who sent it! Hey Emmett!" I shouted.

"Come on out here." I was almost dancing in excitement, and even though I know that big-time detectives don't act that way, I just couldn't help myself. I felt fabulous. This time I had completely scooped Clarice. At last I had found some answers that hadn't even entered her head. "Listen to what I just found out!" I cried.

Then, while they stood staring at me, I told them all about the conversation I'd overheard at the dentist's office. "So maybe this property would be valuable to that shopping mall corporation," I finished. "And Crandell Teeters is trying to buy it cheap before you find out its real value!"

"My heavens!" Mrs. Vickers burst out. "Why, I'll bet you're right, Flee Jay! Emmett, you see? I told you I didn't like that awful man. He had an unpleasant aura."

Emmett was grinning. "Do you think this place has some value, then? Do you really think so?"

Clarice was torn between surprise and disgust. "I should have had my appointment with Attila the Hun today," she mumbled.

I swallowed my impulse to shout "nanny, nanny, boo, boo" at her. Like the air suddenly leaving a burst balloon, my energy was gone, and I felt I needed to collapse. Hot and sweaty, I glanced around for something to plop on. The folding chair I had noticed between the huge desk and the front door was still standing there, so I hurried over to grab it.

"Oh no!" I shouted, stopping abruptly as I reached its front. A black paper covered the seat of the chair. Feeling like someone picking up a dead rattler, I reached for a corner of it and lifted it up. It dangled there a moment, and then it swirled around to show a scrawled white message.

Once again, the words were curled around like snakes while an ugly cobra hissed.

THIS IS MY LAST WARNING!
GET OUT!!!

"Somebody must have come in here, after all," I whispered.

"But that's impossible!" Mrs. Vickers sagged against the counter. "Impossible! I've been standing here the whole time!"

"Well, *someone* must have delivered that message," Emmett declared.

But no matter how much we talked, we couldn't see how anyone could have come through that door.

"I know that paper wasn't there when we came back from lunch," Clarice said. "I checked every inch of this place. And most of the time I've been right out here in this room working. I went back for more soap and water twice, but—"

"I've never left this desk," Mrs. Vickers interrupted. "I came back here to organize our questionnaires. Don't you think I would have seen if anybody came in? I want to get people interested in this club."

"Well, I was in the back the whole time," Emmett declared. "So I never saw a blasted thing."

"Who could have such power?" Mrs. Vickers's rosy face was drawn. Her bells clanked as she leaned forward. "Maybe Mr. Teeters isn't behind this warning at all! *He* isn't invisible. The person who delivered this warning must have been invis—"

"Are you absolutely sure, Aunt Emma?" Emmett's happiness at hearing my news had sloshed into misery. His jogging shoes almost squished as he moved closer to his aunt. "Maybe Mr. Teeters—or that fellow who works for him—came in and you didn't happen to notice. The chair is almost by that front door and—"

"Don't you think I'd notice someone coming in?" Mrs. Vickers's lined face creased into deeper lines. Gray hair poked out from under her turban, and she didn't even stop to pat it back into place. "I want to get customers for you, Emmett. Don't you think I'd jump right up if somebody came through that door?"

"But this isn't logical," Clarice complained. "Nobody can be absolutely invisible."

And suddenly her words made me think of that old forbidden mystery I told you about earlier—the one I started reading at the library when I was a little kid. Nobody knew where the murder victim was in that story, even though he was right inside the snow on the front lawn. He was invisible too, because whenever people looked at him, they saw only a snowman.

I caught my breath. Maybe—just maybe—I crossed over and went behind the desk. There was a small wastebasket by Mrs. Vickers's feet. I was right! A white envelope lay crumpled up at the bottom. "Occupant," it said.

All my detecting antennae quivered, and I knew that this time I'd done the full job. "Crandell Teeters is trying to scare you into selling cheap," I said. "And now I see exactly how he had those notes delivered!"

The Snowman Melts

People see what they expect to see. That's a fact. If a picture hangs in the same spot on a wall for three years, the people in that house will say it's still hanging there, even if you've taken it down. What happens is that once people get used to seeing something, they don't actually see it anymore. They only see what they expect to see.

Clarice and I talked about this once, so that's why I know. In the same way, people may *not* see something that's actually there, because it's so ordinary. I read a story by Edgar Allan Poe where all the detectives in the police department couldn't find a special letter. They only knew it had been hidden in a man's apartment. They tore the whole place apart while they searched, but they just couldn't find it. It turned out that the letter was in plain sight in a letter basket on the man's desk. They didn't see it because it belonged right where it was. It was absolutely ordinary.

So all of those ideas hit me at once when I saw "Occupant" on an envelope in the wastebasket. It was like watching that snowman melt in that old book and seeing the big answer staring right out at me. Who's so ordinary because we see him so often? Who might be so common that he's almost part of the scenery, almost invisible as he walks up and down streets, on and off of porches?

I reached into Mrs. Vickers's wastebasket and pulled out the white envelope. "What's this?" I asked.

Mrs. Vickers waved her hand. "Why that's nothing. Just an ad marked for whoever happened to be living here."

"But who brought it?" I asked.

"Just the mailman," she said. "He brought it in and handed it to me just a few minutes before you came in the—" She stopped; she caught her breath.

"So someone *did* come in!" Clarice cried.

"But a mailman?" Emmett asked. "Would a mailman—"

"He probably wasn't a real mailman," I said. "And I'll bet Mr. Teeters hired him to deliver phoney 'mail' and, if nobody was looking at him, leave those creepy warnings on his way out."

Clarice dropped her sponge. She ran over and grabbed the envelope. "The address isn't even for this building! And if a mailman came by here yesterday too, we might not have even noticed. I'll bet you're right about a phoney mailman, Flee Jay. I'll bet you're right!"

I *was* right. We found out later that Crandell Teeters admitted he had hired someone to dress up like a mail carrier and walk into the health club two days in a row. He was betting that nobody would pay any attention to someone so ordinary, and he was almost right. He thought that Mrs. Vickers was such a superstitious old woman that, after getting those scary warnings out of "nowhere," she'd insist that she and Emmett sell the property for next to nothing just so they could get out.

Yeah, I was right about the value of the land there too.

Emmett and Mrs. Vickers were able to sell the health club to the mall corporation for a "healthy" sum, as I told Clarice, although she never got the pun. Crandell Teeters is going to be tried for extortion or some such thing, because what he did is illegal. The police discovered that he'd used schemes to frighten other property owners into selling too.

"I have to admit it," Clarice told me when all the unanswered questions were answered and we were back at home again. "You did almost as well as I did on this one, Flee Jay." She took the folded shopping list Mom had given to us that morning, and she carefully put it in her purse. "And you know what?" She paused. "You haven't even gloated over how you solved that last puzzle all on your own."

I stared in astonishment as Clarice gave an embarrassed laugh. "I guess I've sort of gloated when I've come up with the right answers in other cases."

I stood up straighter and folded my arms. "Well, I *am* older than you are Clarice. And I'm a lot more mature. After all, only little kids feel they have to brag about the things they can do."

She actually blushed. Then she shrugged and looked at her feet. "Anyway, I'm off to the store now to get this stuff for Mom. Sure you don't want to come?"

I shook my head. "No, I'm going to stick around the house. You go ahead, Clarice. Mom only listed a few things we need for supper. You can manage them on your own."

"Okay." She threw her ugly purse over her shoulder and started out the door. "And thanks again for not chortling about how you solved that last puzzle in the case of the haunted health club."

"No problem," I answered. "You solved some of it, didn't you?" As I shut the door, I collapsed against it in a fit of giggles. I only wished I could have been there in the grocery store when Clarice looked at Mom's shopping list. At the bottom of it, under milk and eggs and alfalfa sprouts, I'd penciled in these happy words:

Nanny, nanny, boo, boo. You can't do what I do.

Well? So I'm not quite as mature as I ought to be. I admit it. But I can still solve mysteries, can't I?
You said it!

From Felice Jennifer Saylor
Girl Detective

HOWLING GOOD FUN
FROM AVON CAMELOT

WEREWOLF, COME HOME 75908-X/$2.75 US/$3.25 CAN

HOW TO BE A VAMPIRE IN ONE EASY LESSON
75906-3/$2.75 US/$3.25 CAN

ISLAND OF THE WEIRD 75907-1/$2.75 US/$3.25 CAN

THE MONSTER IN CREEPS HEAD BAY
75905-5/$2.75 US/$3.25 CAN

THINGS THAT GO BARK IN THE PARK
75786-9/$2.75 US/$3.25 CAN

YUCKERS! 75787-7/$2.75 US/$3.25 CAN

M IS FOR MONSTER 75423-1/$2.75 US/$3.25 CAN

BORN TO HOWL 75425-8/$2.50 US/$3.25 CAN

THERE'S A BATWING IN MY LUNCHBOX
75426-6/$2.75 US/$3.25 CAN

THE PET OF FRANKENSTEIN 75185-2/$2.50 US/$3.25 CAN

Z IS FOR ZOMBIE 75686-2/$2.75 US/$3.25 CAN

MONSTER MASHERS 75785-0/$2.75 US/$3.25 CAN